ALBERT ROSS IS LONELY

Anthony Dalton

Anthony Dalton Books

Albert Ross is Lonely

Copyright © Anthony Dalton 2017

All rights reserved.

ISBN 13: 978-1546543671
ISBN 10: 1546543678

Cover design by Steve Crowhurst
Cover photograph: Man on cliff © Steve Crowhurst
Background scene front and back covers courtesy of Graphic Stock
Horse and rider on back cover courtesy of Shutterstock

Published by Anthony Dalton Books
Font: Garamond 12
Printed in the United States of America

For all the

TRIPPS

&

AMANDAS

&

ALBERTS

May they all find companions.

...And a good south wind sprung up behind;

The Albatross did follow...

From *The Rime of the Ancient Mariner*,
— Samuel Taylor Coleridge

ALBERT ROSS IS LONELY

ALBERT

Late morning. A mantle of thick sombre clouds hangs low over the sea threatening rain. Abusive North Atlantic winds batter the cliff, swirl across the moorland on top and raise the man's clear, waterproof poncho like an errant see-through skirt, revealing the brown leather jacket beneath. Guillemots, razorbills, and kittiwakes cling to their precarious nests on the sheer wall. Gannets and a few Arctic terns ride the disturbed air currents with casual grace. Others fly low, watching the murres bobbing on the troubled surface of the waters between the mainland and Handa Island. A lone black-browed albatross soars into view.

The great bird rockets down a breaking wave, the oceanic turbulence chasing it but never quite catching up. With minute adjustments of its wing tips and tail feathers, the nautical nomad with a white body and dark grey wings glides through the trough between two waves. Close to the sheer cliff, the albatross rises above the stuttering white spray and crinkly wet spindrift. Catching a thermal, it soars far above the angry sea and the nearby craggy headland until it can look down on its home away from home. It turns its head left and right while its eyes, hooded by black brows, take notice of all movements, no matter how small.

A pink squid, the size of a man's hand with fingers spread wide, shows itself near the surface of the sea for a few seconds. It is visible long enough for the albatross to take notice and begin its descent. The squid sees an ominous dark shadow swooping over the water and, before it can react in a defensive mode, the albatross has it in its hooked yellow beak. With a toss of its head, the bird swallows the writhing cephalopod in one motion. Spreading its massive wings, the albatross runs a few paces across the water flapping them to an internal beat to gain lift. Within a few minutes the elegant bird is once again high above the sea, patrolling the alien coastline as it has done for more than four lonely decades.

TRIPP

My opinion of Fate and the often inconsiderate way it works is about as low as it can be. I never expected the tail-end of my life to be like this, or for it to loom on the horizon so soon.

"You have a weak heart," the cardiologist in the Vancouver hospital said. That was the first blow. When I pushed her for complete and honest details she replied, "Mr. Hatcher, the harsh truth is this: you were probably born with a weak heart. It just never showed up until recently. And your hectic lifestyle has not improved it."

I wasn't ready to deal with news of this nature, but I had to ask, "Okay, Doctor, what, if anything, can I do to keep on living my outdoor life?"

We talked for a long time. She said I should slow down, drink less, avoid stress, reduce my physical activities to a more acceptable level – whatever that meant. The final analysis, unspoken but hovering there like a bird of doom, was – if you continue to live at your current pace, don't expect to live a long life. I interpreted that to mean, "If you have things you want to do, go and do them now, but do them slowly." She gave me a prescription for some pills, the universal medical panacea, shook my hand and said, "Goodbye." An awful sense of finality there, I thought.

So, there I was, forty-seven years behind me and, apparently, not as many in front as I had expected. The sudden realization of my mortality was almost overwhelming. I went home enveloped in a mental fog.

"Why?" I asked myself. "Why?" Over and over again. Getting no answers and not expecting any, I ignored the doctor's warning and channeled my personal anguish into activity.

For the next few hours I paddled my sea kayak as hard as I could to circumnavigate the island where I spend most of my leisure time. The exercise didn't kill me, although I suppose I was half expecting it to. All it did was to take away some of the frustration for two hours and wear me out. That happened a lot – getting worn out – losing my breath. Symptoms of a heart that has to struggle more than it should. I stowed my kayak on the rack under my house where it lives when on land, drank a double shot of single-malt Scotch quicker than I should have, went upstairs, threw off my clothes and crawled into bed on the second floor. There I let my feelings flow.

By daybreak much of my sense of self-pity had abated. I sat outside with my early morning mug of strong black coffee watching a great blue heron stalking a meal on the shore-line. That predatory bird showed such extreme patience. It walked a few paces with a silence born of inherited experience. It stood perfectly still for what seemed like hours. When it struck, the thrust of its long beak was slow and deliberate.

Could I do that? I wondered. Could I slow my life down and still enjoy many of the activities that make me happy? Could I teach my mind, my body and my heart to work to a new, slower rhythm? To do so would mean no more racing around the world on hectic magazine assignments with impossible deadlines. It would mean no more trekking through humid jungles. No more stomping around in the mountains. No more riding across deserts. It would mean eating healthier food; cutting down on the Scotch and wine. It would mean exercise without undue strain. It would mean working without stress. It was a tall order: such a tall order. What the heck, I thought. It was worth a try. With the heron as my role model, I determined to do my best. First, though, there were too many distractions in my life and too many interruptions. Too many phone calls. Too many text messages. Too many social invitations. "A change is as good as a rest," someone once said. I was never good at resting. A change of scenery seemed to be required. I needed to get far away.

I have a passion for birds, especially sea birds – the many species that frequent coastlines. That's a big part of the reason why I came here soon after I received the unpleasant news. That's why I came to this barren, rugged, windswept coastline on the North Atlantic side of Scotland's celebrated Highlands. I felt I could be happy here studying the gulls and guillemots, the murres, the razorbills, the acrobatic Arctic terns and the inquisitive puffins. Most of my favourite birds could be found on this coast, such as the many cliff dwellers and the ocean nomads, and the one anomaly – a lone black-browed albatross that should have lived in another hemisphere. And then…well, I never expected to meet a girl like Amanda, especially not at this near terminal stage of my life.

AMANDA

After four long days on the road from my home near Fowey towing the heavy trailer, I was tired. Only the fact that we were approaching our destination kept me going. So many cities and towns had passed. Now, with Inverness – the last city on our route – long since lost from the rear-view mirrors, the town of Lairg would soon be in our sights.

With so many hours of driving, I had had a lot of time to think. Time to think about Rick and his betrayal. Time to think about Clare. That bitch. I wondered if Rick ever thought of me out there under the hot desert sun. I wondered if he regretted leaving me for Clare. Tiny tears prickled at my eyes and escaped down my cheeks. I brushed them aside with the back of my hand. That's all in the past, I reminded myself. It's done. I forced them from my mind to concentrate on driving. It wouldn't do to have an accident now when we were so close to our goal.

My plan had always been to make camp on the cliffs somewhere in sight of Handa Island on the north-west coast. From there I could roam the moors in sight of the sea as far north as Cape Wrath with relative ease. Somewhere along that route I knew I would find the creature I had made the long journey to study. The comforting purr of the Land Rover's engine kept me company as we meandered through Lairg and approached the long, slim ribbon of Loch Shin. Behind me, in the trailer, Djort – my horse – endured the drive in silence.

After a final night sleeping in the Land Rover, in the comfortable bed I had prepared in the back, we arrived on the edge of the popular fishing village of Scourie in the early morning. There I stopped to study my map and to consider the options. Djort thumped her foot on the floor of the trailer to remind me she needed to stretch her legs.

"I'm coming," I called and led her out. Djort nuzzled my neck and breathed into my ear as I stroked her nose. As soon as she was quiet I saddled her and rode up a steep footpath. At the top, we came to a vast open meadow or moorland dotted with thick clumps of heather between the cliffs and a distant hill. The sky was a bleak marbled grey. Handa Island showed in dark silhouette to the north-west. My map told me the hill was Ben Stack. I decided to make camp at its base.

Leaving Djort to graze, I studied the breathtaking scenery for a few moments before running back down the path to my car and started the engine. The Land Rover snarled at the challenge ahead then, growling in second gear and four-wheel-drive, the tough old utility vehicle tackled the rough slope – towing Djort's now empty trailer. As we passed the horse, Djort raised her head and trotted behind her trailer. She seemed to like the moorland, perhaps because it reminded her of Cornwall.

An hour after her our arrival, I had erected my spacious walk-in tent and positioned the Land-Rover and trailer as a windbreak on the weather side. We were far enough away from Scourie for privacy and close enough to the coast for my work. For better or for worse, this would be my home and base camp for the next few weeks, or for as long as I needed to stay.

TRIPP

Our first meeting was not the most auspicious. I heard her coming long before she arrived. She galloped towards me just as I found Albert through my binoculars. She came from well inland, at right angles to the narrow cliff-top path I always take, her horse's hooves thudding through the heather. Without more than a brief glance in her direction, I grunted in annoyance. Even so, I kept my binoculars trained on the distance. I hated interruptions when I was working.

"Hello. What are you looking at?" the young woman asked as she reined in her snorting horse.

"A bird," I answered. I knew it wasn't my friendliest tone but I was not happy to be disturbed. I half turned to her. "Miss, would you, please, either ride away as quietly as possible or get down off that horse? You make an intimidating spectacle up there."

She reacted immediately. Her face straightened. Her lips tightened. "Who the hell do you think you are?" she asked with more than a hint of annoyance. "Do you own this land?"

"No, I don't. Now, please, either go away or get down off that horse. I'll explain in a moment." I took another look at the distant clouds through my binoculars.

She gave a long drawn out, "Oooh!" I guessed she was glaring at me as she dismounted. Patting her horse on the flank loud enough for me to hear, she sent it off to forage on the lush grasses of the moorland.

"Thank you," I said.

"Are you always so rude to people?"

"I thought saying 'thank you' was polite," I replied, continuing to scan the distance.

"That's not what I meant, and I'm sure you know it," she snapped back at me.

I lowered my binoculars and looked directly at her for the first time. She was pretty, very pretty, even wearing that silly black hard hat with a peak like a duck's bill. Just looking at her made my skin feel warm. She radiated energy, and something more…a mix of passion, naïveté, intelligence. She made me uncomfortable, in a special indefinable way. I wanted her to leave. I hoped she would stay.

"Don't mistake my sometimes abrupt manner for rudeness," I told her. "I'm here for a purpose. You and your horse are disturbing the elements of these few moments."

"Oh, you're American," she tried. "I suppose that explains your attitude."

I shook my head, getting exasperated. Taking a slow breath, I said, "Now you are being rude. And, I'm Canadian, not American. Either way, my nationality has nothing to do with what I say to you, or how I say it."

She waited, fidgeting from foot to foot while I continued to study the sea. Then she blurted out, "Look, whoever you are, I'm sorry I've upset you. I didn't mean to be intrusive. I thought perhaps you were looking at that ship out there." She pointed to the north where an oil tanker steamed west in silhouette. To be honest, I hadn't even noticed the ship.

Throughout the winter and early spring, for most of the time, I had been the only person to frequent this narrow path on the windswept, often rainy headland overlooking the North Minch and Handa Island. None of the few other hardy types who passed had shared more than a cursory greeting, "Morning." Or, "Afternoon." None had stopped to chat. None had been invited to. None had interfered in my work in any way, until now.

"Okay. Apology accepted," I said, scanning the sky from one side of the horizon to the other one more time. "My name's Tripp – with a double 'p.' What's yours?"

"Tripp – with a double 'p'? What kind of a name is that?"

"It's my name. What's yours?"

"Amanda – with an 'a' at the beginning and end and another close to the middle."

"Cute. Very cute. Well, Amanda…" I hesitated for a moment and then asked, "You're not a Mandy, are you?" Amanda shook her head.

"Good," I said. "Well, I may as well go home and leave the cliff to you and your horse. He won't come now. You and your animal have made a certainty of that."

"Who won't come? You still haven't told me what you are looking for."

"I told you I was looking for a bird. I thought I saw him out there a few moments ago, but he's gone now."

"You are looking for one particular bird?" Amanda sounded scornful, then added. "How do you know it's a he?"

"I know because I have been studying this particular bird and trying to earn its confidence for many months." I picked up my small backpack of camera equipment and snacks, hefted it over my shoulder and prepared to leave. "No point in staying here now. I'll have to come back later."

I gave Amanda a half salute and started off along the cliff-top path for my home near the distant village.

"Wait," she called, taking fast strides to catch up with me. "I'll walk part way with you, if you don't mind."

She placed two fingers in her mouth and let out a piercing whistle. The horse trotted obediently after her. I stopped and shook my head in frustration.

"Are you always so noisy?" I asked.

"No, as a matter of fact, some of the time I'm very quiet. I think you are being quite unreasonable."

I stopped and looked at her. "I'm unreasonable? You barge in on me like an animated tempest while I'm working, yet you think I'm unreasonable." I shook my head in surprise.

Amanda was about medium height, the top of her helmeted head reaching just above my shoulder. "What's your surname?" I asked.

"Tregower. Amanda Tregower," she answered, offering me her hand to shake. "I'm from Cornwall."

"Well, Amanda Tregower from Cornwall," I said as I took her hand, "it seems you have a strange way of looking at other peoples' situations." I was still holding her hand and studying her eyes. I felt like I was in a trance. She glanced down at our clasped hands and back up to my face again. She flushed and smiled as she withdrew her hand.

"You're not a Mandy? No, you said that. That's good," I continued. "Amanda has some fire in it. You know, I expect, that in literature the name holds wonderful connotations of love?" I looked sideways at her, wondering why I was babbling so much, feeling something akin to an embarrassed smile playing around my mouth. "I think Amanda suits you, although you are too noisy to be lovable, I suspect. Anyway, the formal version is best. Mandy sounds too childish for you, somehow."

A blush fluttered across Amanda's face. Another small smile creased her mouth. Her hazel eyes looked away. With nervous fingers, she tucked a few loose strands of auburn hair under her hat in an attempt to cover her embarrassment. I let go of my binoculars, allowing them to hang against my chest from thin leather straps.

We walked in silence for a while. I took the lead along the narrow path. Amanda followed in my footsteps – the prints from her riding boots joining the countless marks made by generations of domestic sheep and wild deer. Her horse wandered along in her wake. After a few minutes, Amanda increased her pace and caught up, walking beside me, her knee-high riding boots scuffing the grass.

"You're a long way from home. What's a Canadian doing out here on a cliff-top path on the north-west coast of Scotland?" she asked.

"I told you. I'm studying a bird."

"I see," she said. "So, are you an ornithologist, or just a twitcher?"

"A twitcher? What the hell is a twitcher?"

"That's what we call birdwatchers in Britain. Twitchers." She said it with a smile and obvious relish.

I knew she was taking a dig at me and grinned back at her. I shook my head; then I looked sideways at her and explained, "I'm neither. I'm a photo-journalist working on a magazine story. Does that satisfy your curiosity?"

"No. Not yet. You still haven't told me what kind of bird you were looking for."

She really was relentless, but she fascinated me. I stopped walking and looked at her. "If I tell you, will you then stop pestering me with questions?"

"Okay," Amanda grinned up at me, her face lighting up in a smile as bright as a summer sun. "Tell me, and then I'll tell you why I'm here."

I groaned but failed to keep a smile off my face. "I can hardly wait," I said. I lowered my pack to the ground and pointed out to sea. "Somewhere out there is a bird that should not be anywhere near this wild land. He's a black-browed albatross..."

Before I could say anything more Amanda jumped in. "Oh, yes. I've heard of him. That's why I'm here. I'm a zoologist, an ornithologist to be more precise. I'm studying errant behaviour in certain types of sea birds for my doctorate. When I heard about this albatross, I packed up everything and drove all the way here from my home in Cornwall to see if I could find him." She spoke in a breathless rush, the words tumbling out like peas freed from a pod. "I think that makes us kindred souls," she added.

"Kindred souls? You think we're kindred souls?"

"Yes. You know, like two..." she started to explain until I cut her off. "I know what it means, Amanda. Now, tell me," I stared at her. "Are you serious? You really are an ornithologist – a scientist?"

"Oh, yes. I'm serious. And I'm very good at my job."

"You are kind of noisy for someone who claims to be studying birds."

"Not necessarily," Amanda answered with an emphatic shake of her head. "I've always been an exuberant person. I come from a noisy family. That doesn't make me any less professional. And, as I said, I didn't know you were looking for a bird when I saw you back there alone."

I shook my head and sighed. Amanda had no idea how annoying she could be. "Did it not occur to you that I might have been alone by choice. Did it not occur to you that I might enjoy solitude?"

"No, it didn't. I spend a lot of time alone too, but I don't really like it. That's why I take my horse with me. She's good company. I like talking with people. So, I came over to talk with you."

"I've noticed you like to talk. Are you a listener, too, by any chance?"

Amanda laughed, not at all put off by my bluff manner. "You're funny," she said. "I think you are actually enjoying this exchange of thoughts."

"Exchange of thoughts?" I couldn't help groaning at the suggestion. "Is that what this is? An exchange of thoughts? Just what I need, a pretty psychoanalytical ornithologist. What next, I wonder?" I looked out to sea again, hoping to see Albert; half hoping to continue my study of birds; half hoping she would keep talking. I heard a loud sigh and looked back at Amanda. She stood smiling at me with one hand in the pocket of baggy khaki pants, the other removing her hat.

"You think I'm pretty?" she asked, shaking her curls.

"Well, yes. I do. But what's that got to do with our discussion?"

"You referred to me as a pretty psychoanalytical ornithologist," she reminded me. "Pretty! You said. That's a compliment. It's important."

"Well, it, it was only a slip of the tongue," I stammered.

"Ha!" Amanda pounced on my words, "I don't believe you."

I put my backpack down again. "Okay, Amanda the noisy ornithologist who just happens to be pretty," I started. Before I could ask the question framing in my mind, she chuckled and said, "I think you're flirting with me."

I had to look away. I could feel the colour rising in my face. I hadn't blushed since I was a teenager. I coughed, playing for time, and then asked, "Have you ever had a straightforward conversation with anyone, instead of flying off at tangents every few seconds?"

Amanda laughed out loud. "Oh, I hope not. That would be rather boring, I should think." She smiled up at me and added, "You should see your face. I really do think you are flirting with me."

I shook my head, trying to keep my mind on track. "Tell me what you know about Albert. Albert Ross, I mean: the black-browed albatross that has lived along this coast for a few decades."

"Albert Ross? Oh, albatross. That's funny. Clever, too. Did you name him?"

"No. The locals have called him by that name for many years. How much do you know about him?"

"Not much," Amanda admitted. In a serious tone, she continued, "I know he shouldn't be here. He belongs in the far south of the southern hemisphere with the rest of his kind. He'd be more comfortable, I'm sure, cruising somewhere closer to the Southern Ocean, like the Falkland Islands. I plan to stay here for as long as my money holds out and take notes on his wanderings and his lifestyle in as much detail as possible. How long have you been here?"

"Just over a year. I came here late last spring. This is my home now. I bought a croft and I have no plans to go anywhere else."

"What do you do here, apart from watching birds?"

"I'm a writer and photographer. I write. I watch birds. I go for long walks with my cameras. I live a quiet life."

"And then I came along on a horse and made you talk to me, poor chap." Amanda's smile was so genuine, I couldn't be mad at her.

"Do you really think there's enough of a story about just one lonely bird for a magazine article?" she asked.

"Yes, there is. Particularly this bird. I write and illustrate a lot of magazine articles. But this one is special." I stopped, trying to organize my thoughts. This woman disturbed me in a way I had never felt. She was the magnet, I was the metal. To cover my confusion, I did something I rarely do: I spoke of my feelings.

"I've always felt a strange affinity with albatrosses," I began. "You know, don't you, that superstitious sailors believe that albatrosses are the souls of the mariners who have died in the stormy waters of the Southern Ocean off Cape Horn?"

Amanda nodded, her hazel eyes roaming across my face as if recording every detail. She blinked and nodded again. "Yes, l do," she replied. "I know the legend and I know Coleridge's epic poem well, but that's fantasy. It has no place in science. I'm here for a scientific purpose; to study the albatross and document its solitary lifestyle. Have you seen him often?"

"I'm not talking about Coleridge. The mythical relationship between sailors and albatrosses dates back to long before his time." It occurred to me she might not be interested in my thoughts, only in talking herself. I changed the subject as she had done.

"You asked if I've seen Albert often. Yes, I see him regularly, usually close to that spot where we met. He seems to enjoy riding the thermals off the cliff over there. Sometimes I go over to Handa and watch him from there. I was waiting for him when you barged onto the scene."

"Sorry about that."

I didn't respond. I was getting cold and looking forward to a hot tea with Scotch, honey and lemon in my croft. I shouldered my pack again and continued walking. In the distance an old long-wheel-base Land Rover with a horse trailer attached and a substantial tent close by scarred the land in front of Ben Stack. "Yours?" I asked, pointing at the vehicles.

"Yes. I'm camping out on the moors to save money. I just arrived this morning. I was taking Djort – that's my horse – out for a run to stretch her legs after being cooped up in the trailer for my long drive."

"There's a good campground in Scourie with amenities, such as showers, laundry, etcetera. Why don't you camp there? It would be more comfortable."

"Not for me," Amanda shook her head. "Still too expensive and too far away from the area I have chosen to begin my research."

I looked at the lonely campsite. My eyes must have registered my disbelief. I studied the sky over the sea and then over the hills inland.

3"What will you do when the weather turns nasty?" I asked. "It will soon, you know – later today fr om the look of that sky. This quiet spell won't last much longer."

"Oh, I'll be okay. I've camped out in lots of wild places and I did research the weather up here before I left home." Amanda showed nerves for the first time in our brief encounter when she added, "How bad does it get? It can't be any worse than Cornwall, I checked. But, if the weather gets too rough, I suppose I'll have to rent a room somewhere for a few days until it improves. Unfortunately, my research grant is only a small one. It's not enough to cover indoor accommodation expenses. That's why I live in a tent – no matter what the weather throws at me."

"I assume you've never experienced a real northwest coast storm? I can assure you, it is something wild to behold. A front will come in from the North Atlantic — that's the one that's threatening now. The sky will turn cold. Those cirrocumuli up there will pile up, building on each other. Then the wind will come in. That quiet sea out there will come alive and get very angry, with waves crashing into each other and against the cliffs. The spray thrown up will join the rain that will come pelting down. This exposed cliff and moorland will not be a pleasant place to be, I can assure you."

"I have heard tales, but I'm sure they're all exaggerated. We get wild Atlantic storms on the Cornish coast too, you know, and I'm a lot tougher than I look."

"You should take the local stories seriously, Amanda. In Cornwall you probably live in a solid house. The first big gust of wind could tear your tent to shreds out here on the moors. You should think about moving closer to the village where you can find shelter."

"No, I'll be okay here."

"You seem very sure. Or are you just stubborn? And what about your horse. How will that poor beast fare in a real blow?"

"She'll be in her trailer, out of the elements."

"Yes, and probably half scared to death, until the wind turns the trailer on its side. Then what?"

"Do you know, I could very easily learn to dislike you, Tripp whatever your name is," Amanda said through gritted teeth, although her eyes spoke different words.

"Does that mean I'll be able to enjoy the cliff without interruption from now on?" I grinned at her and started to walk away.

"Oh, you are such a...a...," Amanda called after me, then changed subject again, "Why are you called Tripp? Is that your real name?"

"My full name is Craig Tripp Hatcher," I called back. "Tripp comes from my mother's side of the family. I've been known as Tripp since I was a child."

"Well, Mr. Craig Tripp Hatcher, I think you are very rude."

"So I've been told, many times. G'bye," I gave her a slight bow and walked on whistling to myself. Ten or so paces later I turned and said, "Oh, Amanda. I'll be out there on the cliff again tomorrow morning, if you'd like to join me. Perhaps I'll introduce you to Albert – if you promise to be quiet. Oh, and, please don't bring the horse."

Amanda reached down, ripped a clump of earth and grass from the land and hurled it in my direction, followed by a rude oath. The missile sailed over my head as I ducked and laughed.

AMANDA

The wind began to gust in increasing strength in the early evening. By then I was at my folding table writing up my journal for the day in my laptop. I hadn't seen the albatross yet but I had made a useful contact. I wrote, "Today I met the most irritating man…"

And then I stopped. Was that fair? I wondered. Certainly, his attitude could have been improved but, I had conflicting thoughts about the man who called himself Tripp with a double p. Closing my eyes, I could see him clearly. He had stray lengths of dark brown and grey hair fluttering in the wind from under his ball cap. "I don't think I like him," I heard my voice say the words even as I doubted their truth. I remembered I had wanted to reach up and tuck the hair in but resisted the temptation. I also noticed he needed a haircut. He looked fit, although his face was lined, perhaps from countless hours spent looking into the wind – or maybe the lines were from stress. Behind a veil of extraordinarily long lashes, his mahogany eyes had glowed with vitality, only the deep shadows beneath them told of some hidden concerns. I guessed he was close to his mid forties – almost fifteen years my senior – maybe more. Despite his grumpy attitude, like him or not, he had made a positive impression on me. He was obviously intelligent.

Purposeful. Quite funny, actually. Taking myself out of that reverie, I finished writing my notes and shut down my laptop to save the battery.

The wind kept shaking the tent and banging against the Land Rover and trailer. I had a cold meal of cheese and crackers then crawled into my sleeping bag and tried to sleep. The wind, and thoughts of that irritating man, kept me awake for a long time. As he had predicted, I did not enjoy my first night camped out on the moors. Despite the tent being sheltered to a great extent by the Land Rover and horse trailer, the wind was erratic – blowing in strong gusts from all directions. The tent flapped and shook. It vibrated and it hummed. Wrapped in my sleeping bag on a mattress of thick, foamy material on a camp bed, I was comfortable and warm enough, but the unexpected power of the wind that first night worried me. Maybe, I should have listened to Tripp's advice.

The storm passed around 4:00 a.m., leaving a light rain in its place and no more than a gentle breeze to rustle the tent. I suppose I must have fallen asleep soon after. I woke up in a bit of a panic when I heard someone call my name.

ALBERT

Albert Ross rode a thermal in the early morning light, soaring high above the headland off the north coast of Handa Island, his eyes constantly alert for the brief flashes of silver that advertised the presence of fish far below. He adjusted his primary feathers, fanning them out to slow his flight. Far below him the sea was a fantasy of white on black as the wind whipped the tops off waves and dashed them to spindrift. In the distance, to the north-west, a small coastal cargo ship rose and fell with the ageless rhythm of the North Atlantic Ocean. Its bow climbed high, shedding water in a spray of white before it crashed back into the next waves, sending sheets of icy ocean roaring to each side.

Albert angled his wings and lost altitude, turning in a circle as he went, his speed taking him down to the troughs between the waves and there he glided with the supreme grace of his kind, only a fraction above the surface of the sea and in full view of two sailors standing by the window of the bridge overlooking the exposed deck of the struggling ship. Changing direction, Albert rose above the waves and circled the ship to cross her wake. There he again flew low, watching the turbulence to see what it would reveal. His diet was mostly small squid, sardines and herrings, plus shrimp. Captain Fergus

Maclean leaned against the wheelhouse door and watched the albatross through his binoculars.

"So, you're still here, are ye, laddie?" he said. "Why don't you go home where you belong?"

Albert Ross circled the ship once more before flying far along its wake, always on the lookout for food. He continued his search as the ship steamed to the south-south-west, making for a distant harbour on Loch Broom.

The young captain was looking forward to getting his ship into Ullapool and taking a break from the sea at his parents' home in Scourie. He was looking forward to joining friends in a nearby village pub, and to a possible evening or two with Flora, the young widow at the bakery. The current voyage around the north coast from Aberdeen, with stops at Peterhead, Buckie, Wick, Stromness and Kirkwall, had been hard. Before that he had been in the Shetlands, Fair Isle and as far west as Stornoway in the Hebrides. He hadn't left the ship for more than a couple of hours at a time in almost six months and he was tired. Even so, he knew only too well, after a week or so ashore, he would be ready to get back on board and feel the waves beneath his feet again. He was no more than 30 years-old but already he had 15 years at sea behind him, most of that on the world's oceans. When he spoke, which was not often, his soft voice betrayed his Orkney roots.

He had seen the lone albatross a few times. On each occasion, it had circled his ship once or twice before flying above the wake in search of food. The bird, he knew, was almost a local celebrity, being seen by fishermen all along the north and west coast. They called the nomad Albert Ross. As darkness fell, the captain stayed on the bridge, drinking strong tea and thinking about the albatross. Thinking about how lonely it must be – the only one of its kind as far as he knew – for thousands of miles. He understood loneliness. It was a part of his life. Part of his position as captain. He was, he reflected, rather like the albatross: a natural wanderer.

TRIPP

That evening I sat at the table I used for a desk in the warm croft, a peat fire burning in the hearth, a mug of hot tea laced with Scotch close to hand and my laptop open. I was trying to write but Amanda kept intruding on my thoughts. The wind grew rougher and stronger as it whistled under the eaves and buffeted the solid wooden door. The thick stone walls rebuffed the assault with a determination, I knew from experience, no tent could possibly equal. The lights flickered occasionally but stayed on. I hoped Amanda had had the sense to move off the cliff. Long before midnight when the late May storm reached its peak, I was in bed, restoring my heart's energy for the following day. I noted the wind was out of the north-west as I wondered how Amanda and her noisy horse were faring; then a restless sleep took me to a private world.

The storm woke me early. I lay in bed for a while listening to the wind and rain and wondering about Amanda's night on the moor. Later, as I washed and dressed, I tried to put her out of my thoughts. I told the mirror over my wash basin, "She's not my problem. Thank goodness." But I could see her dazzling smile and hear the laughter in her voice. She would not leave my mind. I devoured two pieces of toast, downed a cup of black coffee, filled a thermos with the rest of the pot, added some sugar, and prepared to face the elements, telling myself that Albert could well be flying over the cliff at that moment. The wind was down and the rain not much more than a fine mist as I left home.

Although Amanda's campsite was a long walk from the cliff-top path I frequented, my feet led me on a wide detour towards the lower slopes of Ben Stack. The dark green Land Rover and trailer were there, looking like toy vehicles. Beyond them I could just see the white top of Amanda's tent. It had obviously survived the bluster of the previous night's storm. Djort, the horse, was grazing to the left of the trailer. She appeared to be on a long tether. The wind continued to send gusts across the moor. A light rain shower marched inland towards Ben Stack. It would not stay long. A small patch of blue sky showed on the western horizon. There was no sign of Amanda.

I walked past the Land Rover, noting the engine was cold. It had not been used that morning. The trailer was expertly protected from the wind by four substantial guy ropes and stakes. I nodded in appreciation. Amanda obviously was more experienced at camping out than I had given her credit for. Djort looked at me; went back to grazing. The sides of the tent flapped at the wind. The entrance was zipped closed.

"Good morning, Amanda. Room service," I called.

A sleepy voice answered, "Huh? Who is…? Damn, it's him. Just a minute."

I leaned against the Land Rover and waited. One minute became five. From inside the tent I heard muffled curses. Something fell over with a metallic clang. Another curse. Five more minutes passed. The rustling in the tent continued. I smiled to myself; shook my head, imagining the scene just beyond the flimsy white wall. The entrance zip opened, sounding like a distant express train. Amanda stepped out wearing un-laced hiking boots, khaki cargo pants, and a bright red parka. She adjusted the woollen hat on her head, looked at me and said, "Oh, it's you."

"Yes, it's me. Who did you expect? Bonnie Prince Charlie, perhaps?"

"Funny. Do you want something?" she asked; then added with a smile, "Oh, I see. You were worried about me, weren't you?"

"Not exactly. I just stopped by to offer you some coffee."

"Thank you. I'll take the coffee, although I could have brewed my own, you know." She smiled at me again, her head slightly on one side. "You were worried about me. I can tell. I think you might actually like me a little bit." She grinned, a flirtatious smile of amusement, as she poured the sweet black liquid into a plastic cup and took a sip. I felt my face flush a little. The second time in as many days.

"The coffee's good, and hot; with the right amount of sugar," she said, saving me from my own embarrassment. "Will you have some with me?"

I nodded and she poured a cup for me. We stood there in silence for a moment or two, neither knowing quite what to say. Amanda broke the awkward spell with a theatrical gesture and, "Welcome to my humble abode, Tripp Hatcher. Won't you come in?" Without waiting for an answer, she pulled the flap aside and walked into the tent. I hesitated and then followed.

"It's a bit of a mess," she said as she straightened a fallen chair. The interior surprised me. It could have been anybody's tent, yet Amanda had made the most of what she had and turned it into a comfortable, if temporary home. A few clothes covered the bed. Her riding boots stood together like sentries on duty by one wall. A large Turkish kilim covered the thin plastic floor beside the bed and under a folding table and two similar chairs. A black leather suitcase lay half open on the floor near the camp bed. A closed laptop computer rested on the table.

"The rug is to keep my feet warm," Amanda explained.

I was impressed by the comfort of the layout and said so. Pointing to the two folding metal chairs, I asked, "But, why do you need two chairs when you are travelling alone?"

"Oh, the second one's for you," she replied with maddening logic. "Sit down."

I sat. Sipped at my coffee, feeling more than a little out of place. "It looks like you have everything you need here," I said, waving my hand in a vague fashion around the tent.

"Yes, I have. Even room service, it seems," she laughed and touched her plastic cup against mine.

"You seem to have survived the storm all right. No damage that I can see and your horse seems relaxed."

Amanda wrinkled her nose. "Actually, I was scared stiff. I thought the tent would blow away with me in it. It was just as wild as a Cornish winter gale. How often do you get these storms up here?"

"Quite often," I nodded. "There's no pattern to them. Sometimes we go for weeks without any strong winds and then we get hit again. You can be sure, there will be other storms."

"Even in summer? Well, I'll have to deal with them as they come," Amanda said then changed tack. "How big is the village? I assume that's where you live?"

"I live on the outskirts. I suppose there are at most two hundred people there, certainly not more. Most of the men are sailors – fishermen – you understand. The women look after the homes, chickens, vegetable gardens and the kids. Everyone knows everyone else and they all know each others' business. They are a gossipy lot, but nice enough. They lost interest in me a long time ago. I'm 'that weird writer fellow up in the old croft.' I guess I never do anything to excite their curiosity."

"I wonder what they will think of me, living alone out here by this mountain?" Amanda looked worried.

"Oh, they'll talk about you but no one will bother you. I'll let them know you are a scientist with a job to do.

They will understand that. They've all seen or heard of Albert."

"Is there a pub in the village, one that serves hot food as well?" Amanda had a habit of putting her head on one side when she asked a question. She reminded me of a puppy I had when I was a boy.

"Yes. It's called *The Bonnie Prince*. You'll find it down by the tiny harbour, on the left-hand side. The landlord's a dour chap but his wife is a happy bundle of friendship to all. His name is Georgie. She is Maggie."

"Thanks," Amanda said. "Maybe I'll see you in there sometime?"

"Possibly. I don't go in on a regular basis." I stood up. "Time for me to be going. Don't get too close to the edge of the cliff. It crumbles in places."

I could have stayed talking with her all day. Instead I went to look for Albert.

ALBERT

As the early morning light crept over the land chasing shadows away, Albert Ross floated on the sea a few miles off shore from Cape Wrath dining on the carcass of a large cod. He had seen the injured fish from high above. It was moving in slow motion; not yet discovered by other oceanic predators. Albert's keen eyes had directed him to a significant breakfast feast before the rowdy gulls could stake their claim. He ate his fill, gorging his belly until his appetite was satisfied. He rested there on the sea, riding the waves up and down for a long time until he had digested enough of his meal. Then, with wings spread wide, he began an ungainly take off run. He was soon airborne again and soaring once more over his adopted domain.

Over the next few days he roamed from the steep cliffs of the mainland near Cape Wrath to the Butt of Lewis at the northern tip of the Hebrides. With the wind as his only companion, he soared on to circle the Flannan Isles, where a large shoal of herring kept him busy, along with scores of gannets, gulls and terns. As the wind changed to a westerly, Albert left the gannets, gulls and terns behind and rode with it. He passed the deserted rock outcrops of Sula Sgeir, Rona, Stack Skerry and Sula Skerry until he reached the northern islands of the Orkneys. Off

Westray, where he followed a busy fishing trawler for a few hours, he flew east and south to reach the Pentland Firth. Abeam of John O'Groats he startled four sport-fishermen in a small boat when he glided past at eye level. Soon after, the familiar sheer cliffs of Dunnet Head welcomed him at the western end of the treacherous strait. Ahead were the waters he knew best: the waters off Handa Island and the adjacent land.

TRIPP

I stood close to the edge of the cliff a few days after I met Amanda. My backpack lay on the ground behind me. I had my binoculars up to my eyes when I sensed rather than heard Amanda approaching. I motioned her to stop with one hand.

"Stay back. It's safer," I said, lowering the binoculars and facing her. "You left your horse at home today."

"Yes. We were out for a ride early this morning. She's grazing and looking after my stuff at base. I walked here through the heather," she added. "I noticed a covey of red grouse halfway across. Have you seen the albatross?"

"No, but there has been other action. When I arrived about an hour ago there was a lot of noise coming from the ledge below us. That's where the guillemots hang out. I laid flat on the cliff and looked over to see a pair mating with all the others sort of cheering them on. A bit voyeuristic of me, I suppose, but I hoped Albert might fly over to try and join in the action. No such luck."

"Are the guillemots still there?" Amanda asked.

"Oh, they are there all the time. At least, some of them are. The rest are out fishing."

"I want to see them," she said. Positioning herself face down on the grass she wriggled forward until she could see straight down. "Hold my legs, please," she begged. "I don't want to fall."

She lay there, face down, her legs wide apart, toes of her hiking boots digging in for purchase. The cloth of her pants pulled tight across her rear, emphasizing the shape. I stood transfixed.

"What are you doing?" she asked in a stage whisper, turning her head to look at me. "Stop looking at my bottom and hold my legs."

Feeling more than a little uncomfortable, I knelt between her legs, pulled them closer together and held them in place with my hands on her calf muscles. A muffled voice said something. I guessed she was thanking me. When she stood up again, she grinned at me and said, "That was lovely. It's a grand sight, isn't it?" I nodded, not sure whether she was talking about the guillemots or about my viewpoint. I think it might have been both, based on the way she looked at me.

"I haven't seen you for a few days," Amanda said. "Have you been away?"

"Yes. Did you miss me?"

"Ha! You should be so lucky," she laughed. "Where were you?"

"Oh, so you did miss me," I teased. "I helped a local take his boat round to Badcall Bay two days ago. We saw Albert down there for a few minutes. Yesterday I was out fishing with old Donald. We were off to the north of Handa collecting mackerel. No sign of Albert there."

"About those grouse I saw. Are there many of them in this area?" she asked.

"Yes. Red grouse are common enough here. I see them often."

"Are people allowed to hunt on this moorland?" She sounded worried.

"Yes, but the shooting season doesn't open until mid-August, so you will be safe enough at your camp for the next few weeks."

"I hope you are right," Amanda said, looking back across the heather. Then, "If you are waiting for Albert now, do you mind if I wait with you? I promise I shall be quiet."

I looked around at the barren moors behind us, at the rounded peak of Ben Stack rising further back. I looked at the cliffs close by and the roiling sea beyond. There were no other humans in sight. "If you wish," I said, pleased to have her there, and went back to studying the northern skies.

Amanda waited in silence for a while, but I could tell she was restless. I did not move, apart from rotating my shoulders to follow a speck against the clouds occasionally. The only sounds came from the wind, the waves breaking on the foot of the cliff far below, the cries of sea birds and an occasional sigh from Amanda. She changed her stance, moving closer to my right side. She stamped a foot, explaining, "Sorry. Cramp. My feet are cold."

Wishing she would be quiet, I kept my vigil. "Oh, you beauties," I said softly as a pod of bottle-nose dolphins chased over and through the breaking waves.

"Is it Albert? Where is he?" Amanda asked as she panned across the sky.

"Dolphins" I said, "about there," and directed her binoculars to where I had seen them. Amanda watched them leaping out of the water for a few seconds then sighed again. She shuffled her feet and asked, "I don't suppose you have a thermos of hot tea or coffee in one of those big pockets. Have you?"

I didn't look at her, but answered, "Just because I gave you room service one morning doesn't mean I'm an ambulatory restaurant. If your feet are cold, put some warmer socks on."

"They're back in my tent. It's too far away." Amanda nudged my backpack. "Do you have a spare pair in there?"

"Always. There's a pair in the side pocket. They'll be much too big for you."

Amanda opened the pocket anyway and pulled out a pair of thick wool socks. "I think they'll do," she said. She sat on the grass, took off her boots and pulled the socks over her own. The heel ended up way past her ankle. She frowned at the result, shrugged her shoulders and put the boots back on. "That's better," she said as she stood up and stamped her feet.

"Amanda..." I started.

"What?" she asked, the picture of innocence interrupting again.

"Why don't you do something useful?"

"Such as?" she asked, as if pleased to have some kind of response.

"You could try standing still and being quiet for a few minutes, as you promised," I said without looking at her; continuing to study the low-lying clouds. Amanda stamped her feet, as if marching, and started to ask, "Why...?"

"Dammit. What do I have to do to get any peace around here," I asked, taking a step towards her.

"I'm cold and I'm bored," she moaned, "and there's no sign of the albatross anyway."

She shuffled her feet and looked at me, head on one side, a smile spreading across her face. "Perhaps we could walk along the path together and, maybe, even talk to each other," she suggested.

I lowered my binoculars again and shook my head. "Whatever happened to peace and quiet, and solitude?" I complained.

The problem for me was that I liked Amanda being there, close to me, annoying though she could be. Without thinking of the possible consequences, I pulled her to me, wrapped my arms around her. "I suppose the only way to keep you quiet is to kiss you. That might work."

Amanda got as far as, "You wouldn't...." but I already had. Amanda didn't struggle. She didn't respond. She just stood there with one hand in her pocket and the other holding her binoculars. When I released her, she took a step back and looked at me, a bemused expression on her face that gradually spread into a grin. "So, you are human after all," she said.

"Yes, I am human. No, I am not a restaurant. Yes, I am looking for an albatross. No, I don't like nosy people. Yes, I am a writer. No, I don't like noisy people and, yes, I did enjoy kissing you."

Amanda hooted with laughter, choking off the sound with a gloved hand over her mouth. Her eyes sparkled as she brushed a lock of hair out of her eyes and tucked it under her woolly hat. "Well," she said, with a mocking smile, "I'm glad we got that out of the way. Shall we try it again, or would that annoy you too much, Mr. Craig Tripp Hatcher?"

I shook my head, embarrassed at my actions and annoyed that she knew it. To cover for myself I said, "You know – you really are a pain. But I think I like you anyway." Not knowing what else to do, I returned to scanning the skies. Amanda remained still and silent, for a moment. I looked back at her. She was studying me at close quarters through her own binoculars.

"Not bad looking," she said, as if to herself but loud enough for me to hear, "even for a rude old Canadian. I wonder if he will try to kiss me again."

This time it was my turn to laugh. I took the binoculars from her hand and answered her question with action. "Yes, I said, "I will kiss you again – and again, if I'm allowed. But not now, Amanda. I have work to do."

As I handed the binoculars back to her, she pouted her lower lip and sighed. "Whatever happened to romance?" she asked, shaking her head.

I was busy roaming the clouds from right to left and back again to play the game any more for now. "Come on, Albert. Where are you? Help me find him, Amanda, please."

We stood close to each other for many minutes, both scanning the skies. There was no sign of Albert Ross. Somehow his absence did not seem important that morning

AMANDA

The rain was torrential when I woke up this morning. I worked for a while, fed Djort, worked some more. By mid-morning I was bored, and I was thinking about Tripp, and about his kiss. The rain continued. I put on a sou'wester and saddled Djort. Trotting into the wind and rain, we made our way downhill to Tripp's croft. I knew he had a shelter where the horse could stand out of the weather and hoped he might share a coffee with me. Perhaps I needed to see him again. Tripp answered my knock with a loud, "Come in whoever you are."

"Oh, hi," he said when I walked into the kitchen. His smile was so genuine, I knew he was happy to see me. "Take that wet coat and hat off, Amanda, and hang them on the back of the door."

"Sorry to intrude. I would have phoned but I don't have your number. I was hoping you might feel like company for a coffee break, and I brought your socks back," I smiled at him.

"Sure, I can make coffee. I can't give you a phone number because I don't have a phone. I don't need one. Pull up a chair."

He scooped photographs scattered across the table into a pile and placed them in a large manila envelope. "No bird-watching today," he said. "Not in this weather."

"So, if anyone wants to talk to you, they must come here, or go looking for you. Is that it?"

"Yeah, that's about it," he smiled at me, the lines around his eyes crinkling. "Remember, I came here to get away from modern-day intrusions. That includes telephones."

While he made coffee, I sat at the table. Unusual for me. I suddenly couldn't think of anything to say. I looked around the croft. The kitchen and dining area was small but efficient. No bookcases but lots of books piled on shelves and on a small wooden table in a corner. Framed photographs of sea birds decorated the walls. The floor was covered with a large oriental carpet. An armoire leaned against one wall. A CD player sent waves of soft music into the background. Peat burned in an open fireplace. It felt homey and comfortable. An open door led into a sitting room where a large leather couch, with big cushions at each end, dominated the space. More books. More pictures on the walls. Another colourful carpet on the floor. Beyond that room was obviously the bedroom. Tripp broke the silence as he handed me a cup.

"The washroom, you know – toilet, etcetera, through there," Tripp pointed with a spoon to the right of the kitchen. "I built an addition on to my bedroom when I first moved in. Now I have a small fireplace in there, and I have a modern shower." He lapsed into silence again. I realized we were both nervous.

"There's no car outside. Don't you have one?" As a conversation piece it wasn't much, but it was the best I could do at that moment.

Tripp poured the coffee and joined me at the table. "No, I don't have a car. I don't need one," he explained. "I either ride my bike or I walk. Mostly I walk."

"How do you get to town when you have to go?"

"I walk, or cycle, to Scourie and take a bus from there to Ullapool. The schedule, such as it is, suits me. If I have to go to Inverness or Edinburgh, I take the train from Ullapool."

"Where do you buy your food? Can you get all you need here and in Scourie?"

"Yes, I could, but I don't need to buy much. I grow my own potatoes, onions and some green vegetables here. Bread I mostly get from the local bakery, although I do bake some occasionally. Dairy products are expensive but I like cheese so I make myself afford them. I get cheese at the supermarket in Scourie. I don't eat much red meat, so I avoid that expense."

As I sipped at the hot coffee, he asked, "So, Amanda, how's things at the camp? A little too much weather for you, I suspect." He smiled, but he was obviously taking a dig at me.

"Oh, the weather's okay," I answered. "That doesn't bother me. I just thought you might be lonely, so I came down to cheer you up." I held my cup towards him, put on my best smile and said, "Good health!"

Tripp laughed. I liked the sound. It had a deep, happy ring to it. "I guess I deserved that," he said.

"I wonder where the albatross is right now," I looked up at a framed photograph on the wall as I changed the subject. "That's him, isn't it?"

Tripp nodded. "Yes. That's Albert. I took that last year, in the autumn. I liked it so much I converted it into a digital painting. I'm rather pleased with the result."

"You should be, it's beautiful."

He smiled at the compliment and then said, "I haven't seen him for a while not since…"

"I know," I interrupted. "Not since I arrived with my noisy horse."

We laughed together. Tripp then explained, "I doubt that there's any connection. He has wandered off for days, sometimes weeks, many times before. Watching for Albert Ross is an exercise in patience – as well as peace and quiet." He grinned at me over the rim of his cup.

"Apart from being a writer and a photographer, what else do you do?" I asked.

"Those two jobs keep me busy enough. I don't need anything else."

"Why did you come here to live? Surely not just because of one albatross?" I felt sure, if I kept digging, he would eventually tell me his story. I was right.

"A small coastal town near Vancouver was my home for over thirty years – but I've always been attracted to wild and windy places away from people." He gave a rueful smile and continued, "I guess I'm what people call a loner. I first came here about ten years ago on a magazine assignment, and I felt a real connection to this coast. That's when I heard about Albert Ross. Last year, because of something that happened to me, I packed my bags and came to Scotland. I haven't regretted it for a moment. I have never been happier, or felt better. I think the harsh weather agrees with me."

"Are you planning to leave me hanging, or will you explain what it was that prompted you to leave Canada? Did something happen? Did you do something wrong? Are you an escaped criminal?" I teased.

"No. Nothing like that," Tripp laughed. "Do you believe in God?"

"Wow, that's one way to change the subject. Did I hit a nerve?"

"No," Tripp shook his head. "But, do you believe in God?"

"Yes, I suppose I do, although I'm not a churchgoer. I'm C of E, that's Church of England, but I haven't been to church since I was a child, except for the occasional weddings and funerals."

I felt the frown cross my face as I bit my lower lip and asked, "Why are you asking about God?"

"God, mortality, afterlife, oblivion, you name it. They've all been on my mind for some time," he said. "It's all of that and yet it's more basic, too. Much more basic." Tripp stood up and reached for the coffee pot, hesitating with his back to me. I couldn't see his face yet sensed he was trying to control a deep emotion.

"What is it?" I asked. "Is something wrong, Tripp?"

He put down the coffee pot; turned and leaned back against the kitchen sink. His eyes stared off through the walls into the far distance. He cleared his throat. Clenched and unclenched his fists; put them in his pockets.

"The fact is, Amanda, a couple of years ago I learned I have a heart problem. Some kind of congenital defect that will only get worse. I could have stayed in British Columbia and taken life easy. Despite the uncertain future because of my health, I came here. That's what happened to me. That's why I mentioned God."

I got up, reached for him with one arm around his waist, my head on his shoulder and the other hand on his heart. "Oh, that's not fair," I moaned. "That's just not fair."

"Fairness has nothing to do with it. It's life. Some people live a long time, others not so long. It appears that I'm destined to be in the second category."

He reached up to a cupboard and took out two glasses. Without asking, he poured a couple of shots of Scotch into each and handed one to me. I still had my arms around him. "So," he asked, leading me back to the table, "back to God again. Do you believe in life after death?"

We talked for the rest of the afternoon. Much of it was serious. Much was also the light-hearted bantering that seemed to come so easily to both of us. Inevitably, late in the afternoon, the talk returned to Albert Ross.

Tripp told me of his earliest experiences with large sea birds.

"I first became interested in albatrosses when I spent three weeks roaming the Falkland Islands on a magazine assignment. That was a wonderful adventure for me. I spent days camped beside a black-browed albatross colony on the cliffs of Saunders Island. It was noisy but I loved it, and I got some spectacular photos.

"I went to Cape Horn three times when I worked as a guest speaker on a cruise ship. I also crossed the Southern Ocean to Antarctic waters on two of those voyages. Albatrosses flew beside us most of the time. I spent most of my off-duty hours watching them from the lower promenade deck. We actually had a black-browed beauty land on that deck one day. Then it couldn't take off again due to the obstacles in its way. Our resident naturalist captured the bird in a large towel, with help from me and a steward. Once it had got over its initial panic, the naturalist stood the bird on the rail, removed the towel and gave it a push. The albatross took flight immediately and joined its brethren soaring among the waves alongside. It was a magical experience. I always hoped to go back to Cape Horn and the Southern Ocean some day."

I told him of my early interest in birds as a child rescuing a sparrow from the claws of a neighbour's cat. "The bird died," I recalled, "but that little tragedy started me on the long road to studying birds, as well as other forms of wildlife, and to the life of a scientist."

"What's your scientific analysis of Albert's wanderings along this coast? Why do you think he frequents roughly the same region most of the year?"

"My scientific mind combined with my woman's instincts lead me to believe he's lonely. Simply put, I think he's looking for a mate."

"So, is that why he hangs around near the gannets and guillemots? He's hoping one of them will suddenly turn into a sexy female black-browed albatross?"

The image made me laugh. "Yes, perhaps something like that. According to my research, over the last thirty years Albert has been seen from Dunnet Head in the east to the Outer Hebrides in the west. He was sighted off Sula Sgeir by some fishermen and he's been recorded off North Rona, the Flannan Islands and once on St. Kilda. There was even a possible sighting in the Shetlands. These birds are natural wanderers, but this one is different. He's out of place. We know that, but he's looking for something and it's not just food. I believe the something that's missing from his life is a mate. Did you know that albatrosses mate for life?"

"Yes, I did know that. The locals say he's been here for almost forty years. He must be getting on towards old age by now."

"An albatross like Albert could live for up to seventy years – even more. They have a lifespan similar to ours, though not quite as long. He was probably quite young when he arrived here, so he could still be in his prime. I would love to get really close to him and take some blood samples to find out more about his health and age."

"Well, my dear, you'll have to become a lot quieter than your usual rambunctious self if you want to become Albert's friend. He likes quiet people like me."

I acknowledged the dig with a wrinkle of my nose and a smile. "Yes, I did get the message."

Tripp betrayed his sensitive side when he told me, "Thinking about birds that mate for life reminds me of the saddest yet most inspiring scenes I have ever seen between birds. I was wandering on a beach near Punta Arenas, in southern Chile. Standing in the shallows was a female cormorant with a broken wing. Unable to fly, she just stood there, waiting for the inevitable. A short distance away, looking extremely upset, stood her mate. Every time a gull flew low near the injured bird, her mate rushed to her defense, squawking and flapping his wings. It was only a matter of time before the gulls collected and attacked en masse. There was nothing I could do to help, and I don't like to interfere with nature anyway. I didn't wait to see the end. It was too sad for me. I had to leave, but that tragic scene left a scar in my soul."

Instinct made me reach across the table and place my hand on his. "Yes," I agreed, "nature can be very cruel at times."

We sat in silence for long minutes while he stared off into the distance at something only he could see. Not wanting to disturb his thoughts, I looked at my hand covering his, tightened my fingers a little, gradually released them, slid my hand off his, tracing soft invisible lines of understanding along his veins. Then I broke the silence with, "Have you ever thought about Albert's long flight to reach this northern land? "

Tripp returned from wherever he had been and allowed a smile to crinkle around his eyes and his mouth. "Yes. I was planning to ask you about that. I don't understand why he doesn't fly south for the Southern Ocean. He must know he's in the wrong place. Why doesn't he just fly back the way he came. He must have some kind of a homing instinct for the Southern Ocean."

"No, he could only return to the southern hemisphere by accident. Albatrosses need strong winds to keep them aloft. The calm of the equatorial belt would be an effective barrier, even if he could get that far. In the days of sailing ships the lack of wind in the doldrums trapped vessels and their crews for weeks sometimes when the winds failed. The same thing would happen to Albert.

"I suspect the young Albert was blown far off course by a tropical storm that began somewhere in the northern quadrant of the South Atlantic, probably close to Africa. He could have flown with the storm until it crossed the equator and then he could have been collected by a subsequent storm and drawn far to the north. After that he would have flown along the strong North Atlantic winds, probably feeding himself in the rich Gulf Stream waters, and ended up here in Scotland."

"So, what do you think his future might be?"

"He has no future. Not in any real albatross sense. He can't go home. He can't find a mate here. He's doomed to a lonely old age roaming the north of Scotland until the end of his life."

"That's sad. But, maybe he's a bit like me. Maybe he's used to being alone and happy exploring this wonderful part of the world by himself."

"I'm not sure you can apply an emotion such as happy to a wild creature. But, if it is possible, no, he's not happy. Not if he's looking for a mate. He's frustrated. What about you, Tripp? Are you happy? Really happy, I mean. Isn't there anyone, a human I mean, in your life? Don't you ever think of having a partner?"

"I almost got married once. That was long ago in my twenties. There have been women since. A succession of them, I suppose, spaced quite far apart, but none affected me enough for a permanent relationship. I never really stayed in one place for long enough. Now I'm working on borrowed time so, like Albert, I just keep wandering and enjoying each day as it comes."

"Do you have any friends here, in the village or in Scourie? How old are you, anyway?"

"No. I do know a few people to talk to, but none that I would call friends. I'm forty-eight, for a few more months. Let's talk about you. What are your plans once you have collected all the information you can about Albert? Will you go back to Cornwall and pick up your life where you left off?"

"I'm hoping to get an additional research grant so I can go to the Falkland Islands and then to the southern tip of South America to continue my work. But that's somewhere in the future, once I have completed my studies here."

"What about your personal life? Do you have one?"

"I'll be thirty-one next month. I was engaged to an engineer named Rick. Last year, a few months before our planned wedding, he announced one day that he was leaving – taking a job in Dubai. My best friend Clare went with him. So, to answer your question: No, I have no personal life to return to."

"What a jerk," Tripp muttered. "However, the loss is definitely his. Do you have any family?"

"Oh, yes," I said. "My father is a professor at Bristol University. My mother is a retired chemist and my brother is an engineer. He's working in Bolivia at the moment. And, in case you are wondering, we are all noisy, happy people."

Tripp laughed. "So, mealtimes in the family home must have been lively."

"Very lively," I answered. "We discussed anything and everything and often there would be two or more conversations going at once. Mealtimes at home were always fun."

A ray of sunshine pierced the gloom and sent its signal through the small kitchen window. "The rain's stopped and the sun's starting to shine through," I said.

"Time for me to take Djort for some exercise. Will you be on the cliff later?"

"I should stay here. I have an article to finish on the single-malt Scotch industry. It's for a business magazine in Asia, and the deadline is close. That's what those photographs are for." He indicated the manila envelope.

"Okay. I'll look for Albert while I'm out. Could I...?"

"Yes, please," Tripp interrupted, "Come back later for a glass of wine. I can also offer mulligatawny soup and a sandwich for dinner."

I had to laugh. "See, now you're doing it. Wine and dinner it shall be. How about six-thirty, or seven?"

TRIPP

Much to my surprise, my basic dinner was a success. Afterwards, even though the rain had returned, although only a drizzle, I suggested we take a walk through the village. Sheltering under my umbrella, with Amanda's left arm tucked through my right and her hip touching mine, we wandered down to the harbour. She felt good beside me, almost natural – like a lover, I thought. Two fishermen working on a boat beside a shed acknowledged us with half smiles and a nod of greeting from one. Amanda chuckled and bumped my hip with hers.

"Do you remember that old song?" she asked and then sang, "People will say we're in love."

It seemed her thoughts were moving in parallel with mine. "You have a good voice," I told her. "Do you know the rest of the words?"

"No," she laughed, "Just that line."

We discussed going to the pub for a drink but decided against it when we looked in the window. "Too many people in there," we agreed.

Feeling more and more comfortable with each other, we went back to the croft for a nightcap. And, of course, we talked about Albert. I related some of my experiences with the albatross.

"I have tried sitting on the cliff, staying perfectly still for hours, hoping he would land and come over to inspect me, but, so far, he has not shown that much interest. He did land not far from me, near the guillemot colony, a few weeks ago but just strutted around with his wings half outstretched for about ten or more minutes, and then took off again."

"Strutted around? Do you mean like a kind of dance?" Amanda jumped up, held her arms out waist high and slightly bent, strutted in a circle and waggled her bottom. "Like that? Did he dance something like that? Did he fan out his tail feathers?"

"Very sexy," I applauded and laughed. "Yes, he did all of that, though not as attractively as you, and, I suppose, it could have been called a dance. Why? Do you know what it means?"

"Indeed I do. Albert was showing himself off in the hope that a female albatross might see him and become interested. He was offering a courtship display."

"Well, he was right out of luck. A few gannets and guillemots watched him and a couple of gulls. Apart from that the only witness to his desire was me. Poor fella."

"Normally he would offer that ritual in the early breeding season. He was probably getting desperate as it's late in the year based on his built-in time clock. The eggs would be incubating in the Falkland Islands by now."

Amanda looked at her wristwatch as she spoke. "Gosh, it's nearly ten o'clock. I'd better be on my way. I need my beauty sleep."

She stood up and pulled on her coat. "Thanks for the soup and sandwich, and for the conversation. I enjoyed myself."

She hesitated, as if about to say something else then opened the door. I followed her to the car and waited while she got in.

"See you soon," she shouted.

I stood there watching as the red tail lights bounced up the uneven track to the moorland. Suddenly, I felt lonely. I wanted her to stay.

"Goodnight, Amanda," I said quietly as the Land Rover disappeared into the dusk.

AMANDA

We settled in to something akin to a routine. We'd meet on the cliff-top path most days and study Albert for a few hours, or we'd walk to other parts of the cliff. We greeted each other with smiles, some light-hearted banter and, sometimes, a brief hug. Albert showed up often enough to keep us both interested in our work but he never came really close, until one morning soon after I had joined Tripp. A dark movement against a white cloud caught my attention.

"There he is. There he is." I pointed to the north. A slim shape, just distinguishable as a bird to the naked eye, flew towards us. "That's Albert, isn't it? And he's coming this way. If we stay still, he'll maybe come right to us."

Tripp tracked onto the bird through his own binoculars. "Yes. Yes," he said softly. "I see him."

Albert came in on a silent glide. He made one pass lower down the cliff and a second soon after almost at eye level to us.

"Oh, he is so beautiful," I breathed as the great bird cruised past.

Albert made a wide circle and then glided in from the north-north-east again, following the contours of the coast. He flew in a spiral descent to sea level where he soared between the waves disintegrating at the foot of the cliffs for a while and then, breaking out of a trough, he rose in silent splendour on a thermal. We had lost sight of him when he surprised us by appearing directly in front of where we stood, only a few wingspans away. He rested there on the wind, using no more than subtle adjustments of his wing tip feathers to maintain his position.

"He's looking straight at us," I said to Tripp. I was amazed and enchanted at the idea of the bird watching us.

"Yes, he does that a lot. I often think he's as curious about humans as we are about him and his species. But he won't come any closer. He never does."

Later we went looking for grouse. That walk across the moorland turned into a discussion about food. "You said you rarely eat red meat," I reminded Tripp. "You sound like an almost vegetarian."

"Not at all. I love chicken and I eat a lot of it. I get that locally. I also go fishing with one of the villagers occasionally. I don't get paid but he lets me keep a couple of cod, ling or pollock each time, sometimes even a small halibut. And I can have as many mackerel as I can carry. Fortunately, I really like fish. I could eat it every day."

We walked side by side. We both had our hands in our pockets, yet managed somehow to lean against each other. As we circled towards my camp we disturbed a few grouse. "Probably the same covey I see most days," I said.

When we reached my camp, and before I could invite him in for a tea or coffee, Tripp said, "Well, here you are at home again. Time for me to get back to writing."

"Yes," I agreed. "I have work to do as well." I reached up and kissed his cheek. "Thanks for the company," I told him. "Perhaps we can do this again sometime?"

"I'd like that," he said as he walked away, taking long strides. He turned once to wave. He knew I was there, waiting for some kind of sign. I waved back, wishing he had stayed for...I don't know. Anything. I just wish he had stayed longer.

"Why am I so attracted to this man?" I asked myself over and over.

TRIPP

I decided it was time to visit Handa Island again. It was as good a place as any to watch seabirds in general and for Albert Ross in particular. The weather forecast for the following day looked reasonable, so I walked into the village and arranged for a ride over the next morning. Feeling sure Amanda would welcome the opportunity of the excursion, I walked out to her camp and interrupted her washing her hair in a bucket.

"Good timing, Mr. Hatcher," she greeted me. "Give me a few minutes to rinse off this soap, please."

"Would you like me to throw a bucket of water over you?" I offered.

She wiped soap away from her eyes and made a face at me. "No, thanks," she said. "That's a job I can do for myself."

I leaned against her Land Rover while she poured a bucket of clean water over her head. "That water's cold," she said wrapping her dripping head in a towel. "Is this a social visit, or are you here for a purpose?" she asked, then continued, "Do you like my new hairstyle?" She took off the towel and shook her head. The sun caught her wet auburn curls and made them sparkle. Having just been washed, the effect was untidy yet so sexy

"You look good to me," I answered. "I'm going over to Handa tomorrow morning for the day. Would you like to go with me?"

"Yes, please. Oh, could I leave Djort in your garage for the day? I have a bale of straw for him."

"Okay. I'll leave you to your beautifying. See you at my place no later than eight tomorrow morning." I walked home feeling quite elated.

We left the harbour on time the next morning. Amanda sheltered from the cold wind behind Donald, the boatman. She eyed the two backpacks I had stowed on board and looked at me with a question on her face.

"Later," I shouted. "When we get there." I pointed to Handa. Amanda nodded and crouched lower.

As we stepped ashore onto a rough-looking wooden jetty, Donald said, "I'll be back about five o'clock, if the weather holds. If not, then as soon as I can."

Amanda had an immediate question for me. "What are we carrying in these packs? We're only here for a few hours."

"Sleeping bags. Basic cooking equipment for camping. A small tent and some freeze-dried food. You never know when the weather will turn against you. I like to be prepared for emergencies," I explained.

"Just like a real Boy Scout," Amanda laughed with a hint of mockery.

I smiled at her, refusing to take the bait. "We'll leave the tent and cooking gear up here out of reach of the tide. We'll take everything else with us. I have sandwiches in that pack for lunch and cookies for snacks, plus a couple of bottles of water."

"You think of everything. Don't you?" Amanda blurted out. Seeing my change of expression, she immediately apologized. "Sorry, I didn't mean that to sound so sarcastic."

Ignoring the slight offense, I responded, "Yes. It's important to do so out here. Survival should be based on preparation, not on luck."

Amanda pursed her lips and frowned for a moment then she smiled and apologized again, "I am sorry, Tripp. That was rude of me. I can see you really do know what you are doing. I'm a bit out of my depth here."

"I know. You'll be okay," I smiled at her, offering reassurance. "Now, you carry that pack. I'll take this one. We have about an hour's walk to the cliff where the birds nest. Let's get moving."

With me in the lead and Amanda following, we made our way up the steep path to the top of the cliff. It was hard going for me. I found I had to stop for breath more often than I had on my last visit. If Amanda noticed my discomfort, she kept it to herself. By the time we reached my favourite site on the other side of the island, we were both sweating. Amanda began to strip off her windbreaker, and a couple of sweaters and tied them around her waist. I did the same, but put my windbreaker back on.

"Thank you for not commenting on my ungainly striptease act," Amanda grinned.

"Actually, I didn't notice," I answered without thinking. "I was busy setting up my camera and tripod."

Amanda's face straightened. A hurt look passed over her. Her smile returned when I asked, "Did I miss anything?"

"You really are a beast," Amanda laughed as she followed my example and replaced her windbreaker. "No, you didn't miss anything. Next time I'll try harder – maybe to music."

The good-natured bantering ceased as a noisy flock of gulls wheeled around over the headland. Terns and gannets appeared, the latter screaming out of the sky like a squadron of dive-bombers to feed on a shoal of herring just under the surface. Within seconds the sky became a backdrop for an aerial display such as I had never seen. Birds flew left. Birds flew right. Birds flew up to gain altitude. Birds flew down and speared the water with vicious accuracy. The metallic surface of the sea turned into a battleground as the aerial predators rocketed in a vertical frenzy to feed on the succulent targets schooling past.

"Incredible," said Amanda, watching through her binoculars. "Absolutely incredible."

While I moved along the cliffs taking photographs and making notes, Amanda spent her time searching for any signs of an albatross. We both became so engrossed in our work that neither noticed the change in the weather until a sudden burst of wind battered the cliff. I looked up at the sky in alarm, turning in a circle to take in the full effect.

"There's a big storm moving in, Amanda," I shouted. "We have to get out of here. Come on, quickly now."

We hiked back to the jetty on the other side of the island as fast as we could. I was disappointed to find my heart and lungs let me down again. By the time we reached the jetty, I was breathing hard and almost doubled over; my distress obvious. Amanda held on to me as I fought to regain control of my struggling body. When I recovered enough to speak I looked at the white water streaming past.

"There's no way Donald will be coming out here to get us in that sea," I groaned. "We'll just have to make a shelter and wait for the weather to improve. We'll settle down in that gully over there. Give me another minute while I get my breath."

Picking up one bag and with Amanda taking the other, I led the way to a slight depression in the land. "We can keep out of the worst of the wind here. Help me with this," I pulled a folded tent out of one of the bags. "Hold tight to the end so it doesn't blow away while I secure it."

"You don't really expect me to get in that little tent with you, do you?" Amanda asked.

"You have two choices, Amanda. You can stay out here in the wind and rain or you can stretch out in the tent with me. That's it. I'm getting out of this wind." Without waiting for her reply, I wriggled feet first through the opening. My legs, body and head followed. Amanda hadn't moved so I zipped up the entrance. She crouched out of the wind in the lee of the tent and swore.

"Damn you, Tripp Hatcher," she shouted. She unzipped the tent and threw herself in head first, landing half on me and half on a sleeping bag. She found herself with her face at my feet and her feet in my face. As I zipped up the tent again, we both started laughing. I unlaced Amanda's boots and pulled them off. "Just so, if you kick me in the head again, it won't hurt as much," I explained.

"This is not a very lady-like position," grunted Amanda as she curled into a ball before stretching out again with her head at the same end as mine. I was still laughing softly.

"Did you plan this?" Amanda asked, grabbing my head between her hands and staring into my eyes. "Did you?"

"No. I have no control over the elements. Now, I suggest you stop attacking me and slide into that sleeping bag for extra warmth. We might as well sleep this through."

Seconds later, while Amanda was still trying to get comfortable, I fell asleep, probably snoring in a gentle parody of the wind. I slept, Amanda could not. She wriggled around in the limited space of the down-filled cocoon and, as she told me later, she wished she had stayed on the mainland.

Amanda woke me in the middle of the night by asking, "Are you awake?"

"I am now. Is there a problem?"

"I'm hungry," she complained.

"There are two bars of chocolate and nuts in the side pocket of my backpack, if you can reach it. One of those should keep you alive for a while longer. I'll have the other one."

"It's still dark outside. Where are you going?" Amanda asked later as I slithered out of the tent.

"To the left," I replied. "You can go to the right. Put your boots on first."

Amanda thought for a second. "Oh, I see," she said as she recognized the call of nature in herself.

This time I suggested that Amanda return to the tent first and get herself settled. When she announced herself comfortable, after much rustling and giggling, I removed my boots and slid with practised precision into my sleeping bag, zipped up the tent and said, "Now, try to sleep for a while." With that I turned my back to her.

"Why? Do I make you nervous?"

"Yes. Keep still and go to sleep."

"I knew it," Amanda spoke softly, but loud enough for me to hear, "he really does like me."

She tried to move away so there was a gap between our two fully clothed bodies. Enshrouded in sleeping bags though we were, the proximity was disturbing to us both. The narrow tent, designed for one person, did not permit the luxury of personal space. Amanda muttered, "Oh, what the heck," and put her back up against mine for the extra warmth. I lay there in silence, all too aware of the delightful curve of her bottom pressed against the small of my back. I wanted to turn and wrap my arms around her, to hold her close, but I didn't dare. Instead I forced myself to sleep until the day began to break. When I awoke there was silence, apart from a light snuffling beside me. The wind had died. Hopefully the seas had subsided as well.

I managed to slide out of the tent without waking Amanda. The sky was clear, only a few clouds up high. The early morning light was almost perfect for photography. Leaving Amanda to her dreams, I hiked up the path to the cliff again, my camera around my neck. I was up on the hill, near the north corner, watching some guillemots feeding when Albert suddenly appeared in front of me. I'm not sure who was most surprised. He rode up on a thermal and came face to face with me. He hovered there on the air current, looking right at me. He was no more than two metres away. The dawn light was perfect, and he was so close I could hardly focus properly. Amanda would have loved it, but she was still sleeping. Halfway down the path from the cliff I met her coming up.

"Good morning," I said, my smile its own greeting.

"Where the heck have you been?" she responded, sounding more than a little snappy. "I've been calling you. I was worried you might have…"

"Nothing to worry about," I interrupted, pointing back. "I was up there," I explained, "talking to Albert."

"I woke up and you weren't there and I was worried about you, and a bit scared too," she babbled. "Sorry I snapped," she made a wry face. "I was worried. Did you just say you've been talking to Albert? Where is he? Why didn't you wake me?" She threw a gentle punch at my shoulder.

"Well, is this your habitual morning personality? Not very friendly. Come on, we have to get ready for Donald to collect us."

I continued down the hill leaving Amanda staring after me. "Wait," she called. "What about Albert? Where is he?"

"Oh, he's gone fishing. You're too late. Hurry up. We have things to do."

Amanda ran to catch up. As she helped roll the sleeping bags and stuff them into the backpacks she bombarded me with questions, "Where did you meet Albert? Why didn't you wake me? Did you get any photographs?"

"Yes. Lots. You won't believe some of these," I showed her the replay screen. "Look at that one."

Amanda gasped as she looked into Albert's eyes. They appeared to be concentrating on her alone. "Wonderful. Show me the rest, please," she begged.

I looked across the strait. There was no sign of Donald's boat. "Okay, you can move from one image to the next with this button."

While Amanda looked at the photographs, I walked back up the path a way to watch for our ride back to the mainland. We waited for a long time. It was midday before the motorboat came in sight, ploughing through the waves.

"Here comes Donald," I pointed to the boat. "Let's get ready."

We were on the jetty and waiting when Donald slowed and guided his boat towards us. "Get ready to jump in as soon as he comes alongside," I shouted.

Amanda tensed and at my signal she jumped, landing in a heap behind Donald. The two backpacks landed beside her followed by a thump as I hit the deck and braced myself against the wheelhouse for support. Donald didn't wait. He put the engine in reverse and backed away from the hazard of the jetty as fast as he dared. His grey-blue eyes, set deep in lines and creases, took in every nuance of the waves as he turned the boat for the crossing to the mainland.

"A wild night, Mr. Hatcher," Donald said without a hint of humour in his rasping voice.

I wasn't sure whether he meant it as a double entendre or not. If it was, I chose to ignore it. "Yes. It was. I didn't see that storm coming until it was too late."

"On the other side of the island, were you?"

"Yeah. We were on the cliffs. The wind came from the north-east very suddenly."

"Aye. It did that. Yon strait kicks up rough verra quick in a blow. I came out for you as soon as I could."

AMANDA

I didn't see Tripp for three days after our adventure on Handa Island. I knew he was busy so I explored alone, riding Djort along the coast in each direction looking for signs of Albert Ross. When I got home late on the third day, Tripp was walking towards me from his favourite spot on the cliff.

"Hello, Djort," he greeted us. "How's your pretty rider this evening?"

I couldn't have kept the smile off my face if I had tried. As I dismounted I answered, "We are both well, thank you, sir, but tired. It's been a long day."

Tripp grinned at me. "Does that mean you would prefer to stay here this evening and eat whatever you eat, or would a dinner in the pub appeal to you. My treat."

"Give me half an hour to get ready and I'm your girl," I said.

"Are you, indeed. Lucky me." Tripp blew me a kiss and said, "I'll meet you at the croft when you are ready. Take your time."

I debated whether to wear a skirt or jeans. Preferring to ride Djort and leave him at Tripp's croft, I chose the jeans. It was, after all, I reasoned, a night in the pub. Not like a real date.

Over dinner, Tripp told me of his immediate plans. "I have to go to the hospital at Edinburgh tomorrow for some tests on my heart. I'll probably stay a few more days as I want to do some research at the university while I'm there. You are welcome to stay here in the croft and look after the place for me, if you want to. There's room to park your Land Rover and trailer. And, of course, there's the garage stable for Djort."

We talked until closing time, interrupted only once when a young sea captain came over to introduce himself and tell us about seeing the albatross foraging in his ship's wake a few times. It was useful information for me and for Tripp. When we walked back to the croft, it seemed natural to link my arm through his. Over coffee and brandy, we talked some more. Exhausted, I fell asleep on Tripp's couch. He must have put a pillow under my head and covered me with a blanket because I woke in the night feeling warm and comfortable, and wondering where I was.

Tripp was gone when I surfaced in the morning. I awoke to the enticing aroma of fresh coffee and an empty house. A note on the table said, "Good morning, sleepy head. Make yourself at home. See you in about a week." A front door key was attached.

Typical of Tripp, he had left in silence and walked across the moor into Scourie to take the bus from there to begin his journey. The croft felt so bleak without him. I looked in his bedroom. The bed was made and all was tidy. A note on one of the pillows invited me to, "Sleep here, if you wish, Amanda." He had added a cute smiley face. Taking advantage of the opportunity, I stripped off and had a hot shower, aware that he too had stood naked in the same place. Refreshed, I dressed, ate a piece of toast and jam, poured a coffee and went to check on Djort.

The first two days dragged. I found myself looking for Tripp on the cliff, even though I knew he was in Edinburgh. "I really miss that man, Djort. I really do." I told my horse every day, and I told Albert when he flew past. Despite my sudden loneliness, and my concern for Tripp's health, I had work to do. I spent at least two hours each morning working on my laptop, and the rest of the time either doing camp chores or studying the prolific bird life of the area. I did not go back to the croft until the end of that week, and then only to leave a message.

TRIPP

The research room at the University of Edinburgh was quiet. Under normal conditions it would have been an ideal place for a writer to work, but I could not concentrate. The angiogram I had endured, and the cardiologist's subsequent words kept coming back, dominating my thoughts. "Your heart is in extremely poor shape, Mr. Hatcher. We need to get you scheduled for a valve replacement operation as soon as possible, and you need two stents. One of your arteries is about seventy-five percent blocked and another almost the same."

"This is not good timing for me, Doc," I had told him. "Let's get this done as soon as possible. I believe I have a lady in my life now. I need to be fit."

"Nature doesn't seem to take much notice of personal timing, Mr. Hatcher. So, let's focus on getting you through the next few weeks. Look after yourself. Don't do anything strenuous. After the operation you'll have a lot more breath and energy. You'll be contacted with an appointment as soon as it can be scheduled."

The cardiologist had then shown me the problem areas on a chart and explained the procedure to repair the valve and to increase the blood flow through the arteries in my heart.

I wasn't even out of my forties, I reflected, yet I had a life-threatening problem. Knowing there was nothing I could do about it and that worrying would only exacerbate the situation, my natural pragmatism won through on the journey home. Soon after leaving Edinburgh, I fell asleep thinking of Amanda. The long train rumbled past the historic battlefield of Culloden, where the Duke of Cumberland's forces had defeated Bonnie Prince Charlie, and on through Perth and into the Grampian Mountains. I missed it all. I awoke when the train pulled into Inverness, where I had to change to another train to cross the Highlands to Ullapool.

I slept again on the second train, only waking when it lurched to a stop at its destination. The bus was outside and soon I was crossing the moors to home. I wondered if Amanda would be there.

The croft was quiet when I arrived near mid evening. The stable empty. Disappointed, even though Amanda had not known my return date, I ate a sandwich and went to bed. There was a note on my pillow. It read, "Thanks for the offer. I decided to wait until..."

With that enigmatic message in the forefront of my mind, I fell asleep.

I was waiting at the harbour early next morning when the fishing boats came in. A few women waited with me, scarves over their heads and wicker baskets on their arms. A noisy flock of gulls whirled around the fleet diving for any scraps thrown overboard. As the first boat tied up, the women descended on the crew in force, determined to get the best fish for the lowest price. I called out to an acquaintance, "Good morning, Andy. I need six good-sized mackerel."

With dinner organized and on ice in my kitchen, I went in search of Amanda.

AMANDA

Tripp came striding across the moor towards my camp as I prepared to go shopping for food. I leaned against the door of my Land Rover and grinned at him.

"Hello, handsome," I said. "What brings you out here?"

He stopped a few paces away and grinned back at me. "I was hoping to see a lady," he said, his hands in his pockets. "Have you seen one around here?"

"Why don't you come closer? She might be hiding in plain sight."

Tripp stood with his feet apart. Taking one hand from his pocket, he crooked the index finger in my direction. "Come here," he ordered.

I shook my head and pursed my lips. "No, thanks," I said, "You might be a dirty old man with evil intent."

He laughed and took a step towards me. I stood up straight and moved one pace forward. "Yes," he said. "I just might be a dirty old man." He held out his arms to me. "Care to find out?"

I couldn't play the game any more. I ran the few paces between us and accepted his embrace. "I missed you, Tripp," was all I could say as I wrapped my arms around his waist.

He ruffled my hair and breathed into my neck. "I missed you too, Amanda."

We stood that way for many minutes. When I looked up at him, hoping he would kiss me, he was staring over my shoulder, his eyes crinkled. "The grouse season has started," he said.

I turned and looked beyond my camp. Far off to the right a line of men and dogs walked across the moor through the heather. A covey of grouse took alarm and fluttered into the sky. Distant guns barked and two birds fell to earth as the dogs raced for them.

"They know your camp is here. They won't come this way," Tripp said.

"I hope not. I was about to drive in to Scourie for some shopping. Will you take Djort to your place? You can see she doesn't like those guns." Noticing Tripp's expression, I added, "She will walk with you if you don't want to ride."

Tripp took Djort's reigns in one hand. "Of course," he said. "If you'd like a good home-cooked meal instead of camp food for a change, I'll be grilling a few mackerel this evening. And there'll be boiled new potatoes and mushy peas."

"We're having mushy peas? Where did you learn about them? They are my favourite."

"A lady recommended them in the fish shop in Scourie when I first arrived last year. I bought a tin. I tried them. I liked them. I'm glad you approve."

"What about your heart? What did the doctor say? Are you all right?" The questions suddenly poured out of me.

"I'll tell you tonight over dinner. Come straight to my place from Scourie. I'll have the wine ready."

* * *

When I arrived in the early evening Tripp was cooking the mackerel on a home-made barbecue in the garden because, he explained, "It keeps the fishy smell out of the house. I love fish but not the lingering cooking odours."

While Tripp set the dining table once the fish were almost ready, I moved a thin stack of three manila file folders on to a chair. The top one bore the title Albert and Eddie in thick black ink. My curiosity was about to open the folder when Tripp spoke.

"Will you have a glass of wine?" He held up a bottle. "It's an Italian sauvignon blanc. A bit rough, but quite palatable and it's chilled. It goes well enough with mackerel."

I put the files down on a chair and sat at the dining table. "Thank you. That would be lovely."

Tripp served dinner without fuss. Watching him, there was no sign of anything wrong with his health. He gave me a smile as he sat and said, "Okay, Amanda, you have been very patient. This is what the doctor said." He explained about the faulty heart valve and the need for stents to open his arteries.

"When is all this supposed to happen?" I asked.

"Soon, I expect. I hope to know within a week or so."

My facial expression must have betrayed my anxiety because he reached over and held my hand. "Don't worry. Everything will turn out all right. Now, let's enjoy the meal and talk about Albert."

We lingered at the table long after dinner was over. Our habitual daytime banter was missing. In its place was a comfortable warmth of togetherness. We talked about birds, about art and about Albert. Tripp asked about the anatomy of an albatross's head, so I sketched the head and beak and pointed out the various parts. Tripp interrupted with, "That's an excellent sketch. You're a really good artist."

"I need to be. I'm a terrible photographer. I either cut the heads off my subjects, or I cut off their legs."

"I'm just the opposite. I'm a good photographer but have no skills at drawing or painting."

I pointed to a close-up portrait of an albatross on the wall. "That's Albert Ross, isn't it? How did you get so close?"

"I took that with a long lens and a tripod as he cruised past me a few times one day. I have a series of quite good images from that encounter."

Late in the evening, as we washed and dried dishes together, Tripp yawned. "Sorry. It's past my bedtime," he explained.

"Mine too," I agreed, with some reluctance. "I'm ready for bed."

We walked to the door together. As he opened it for me, I stopped and said, "Tripp, I..." It was as much an appeal as the beginning of a statement.

TRIPP

The rain woke me early. I stayed in bed, studying the tousled head asleep on the pillow beside me. Close up I could see strands of red and gold among the dominant auburn. Amanda's decision to join me in bed had been as a much a surprise to me as it appeared to be to her. Although I wanted her to stay, I had thought she was about to leave when she changed direction, took my hand and said, "I hope you don't mind," as she led me to my bedroom. Now, with the morning chill on the air, the warm body beside me felt perfectly natural. I watched her for a while until a hazel eye opened and peered through a tangle of unruly curls at me.

"Good morning," Amanda said, her sleepy smile playing on her mouth. "Is this what you meant when you invited me to use your bed?"

"For me that was wishful thinking. This was a lovely surprise."

"It's a lovely way to wake up, too," she yawned. "Much nicer than on Handa."

Amanda looked into my eyes, resting her elbow on the pillow and the palm of her hand against her face. "I must say, Tripp Hatcher, if you have a heart problem, I can't begin to imagine what you were like when you were younger and really fit." She giggled and stroked my chest.

She was quiet for a moment and then, with her voice almost a whisper, she said, "I hope you get well soon. I like you very much. Far too much."

Unwrapping my arms from around her, I said, "If you like me so much, what are you doing lazing in bed? What's for breakfast?"

With a shout of laughter, Amanda kissed me, leapt out of bed and, standing naked before me, she saluted. "Yes, sir! First, I need to get dressed, sir! It's bloody cold in here. My extremities are freezing. Look!" She pointed to her nipples. "Why don't you do something useful, like lighting a fire to warm this place up. I'll get the kettle on."

Over a breakfast of buttered toast spread with a thick layer of local marmalade, and steaming mugs of tea, we smiled at each other a lot. At some point I asked, "That wasn't just a one-night stand, was it? At least, I hope it wasn't."

"Would you like me to stay tonight and prove it to you," Amanda grinned back at me as she held a piece of toast near her mouth.

"I would like that very much," I replied. "If you're not too busy, of course."

"Oh, good. I was planning to anyway. Cold as this croft can be at times, it's a heck of a lot warmer than my tent, and …"

She had said enough. I stuck my index finger in the marmalade jar and smeared a sticky sweet layer over her lips, saying, "Shhh."

Amanda held on to my hand as she licked her lips and then sucked the remainder of the marmalade off my finger, all the while watching me with a half smile on her face. Trying to keep my grin under control, I chuckled and said, "Later, woman. I have work to do. Let's go find Albert."

That day, for the first time, we acted in harmony as we waited for Albert Ross to join us. Amanda smiled a lot and leaned against me at times. She reached for my hand, stroked it and she remained quiet. I did my best to ignore the dull ache in the region of my heart. For the moment, I was happy and at peace. When the wind swirled around behind us to blow from the land, I moved Amanda in front of me and held her there out of the wind, her back against my front and my arms across her chest, while we watched for our favourite bird.

"I waited for you for so many years," I whispered into her hair. "You took such a long time to get here. I feel like it's almost too late."

Amanda turned around in my arms. "Don't say that. Don't you dare say that," she said, part pleading; part angry. "We are here. We are together. This is happening now. That's all that matters."

We stood wrapped in each other's arms in silence for a long time until Amanda said, "I'm too comfortable to move. Let me know if you see Albert."

"I'm not really interested in Albert today. I have all I want right here."

"Me too."

"I've been thinking…," I started.

Amanda cut me off with, "Do you want me to move in with you?"

"You're interrupting again. I was about to say that you would never survive the coming winter in your tent, especially up here on the cliffs," I explained.

"I know, but you do want me to move in with you?" Amanda persisted.

"That's what I was trying to say before you cut me off."

"I know." Amanda turned and kissed me. "I would love to."

"If you do move into the croft with me, everyone will know – in the village here and in Scourie. There are no secrets in small communities."

"We've already spent a night together over on Handa. Half the people on this coast and everyone in the village must know about that by now."

"They do and they enjoy gossiping about it and imagining what happened over there. They also will have heard you stayed with me for a night a few weeks ago – innocent though it was. By now, many of them will already know you spent most of yesterday and all last night in my croft. There are nosy eyes everywhere."

"Good. Now we'll give the locals some extra juicy gossip to chew on," Amanda laughed. "I'll go and pack up my tent and things."

"Do you want my help?"

"No, thanks. I can manage."

"Okay, I'll be here on the cliffs somewhere, waiting for Albert."

She bumped me with her hip and walked away singing, "People will say we're in love."

Albert Ross flew in between the waves as Amanda drove her loaded Land Rover and trailer along the cliff and down the hill to the croft. She was too busy concentrating on the narrow track to notice what was happening at sea. I hoped she was too busy to notice I was in pain. It only lasted for a few seconds but I knew it was another warning.

* * *

By the time I got home after watching Albert soaring among the waves with the gulls and guillemots, Amanda had moved in. Her tent was packed in the Land Rover. Djort was in the stable. Amanda was in my – our – bedroom putting a few clothes away.

"I made some space for my things in the wardrobe. Is that okay?" she asked.

I felt tired, yet happy. "That's where they should be," I agreed. "Now, I need to rest for a few minutes."

I lowered myself into my easy chair and fell asleep. Unknown to me, Amanda continued to potter about the house, quietly, it seemed, without waking me. I stirred in the late afternoon to see her sitting opposite me, a mug of tea in her hands and a smile on her face. "Hello," she said. "Feeling better?"

By the time we went to bed, having her in the house seemed natural, although with the kitchen area so small, we bumped into each other a few times. I slept well that night, sated by love. In the morning, wrapped in each other's arms, she said, "Tell me a story, please."

I thought for a moment and then started, "How do I love thee? Hmm. Let me count the ways…" I paused and studied Amanda's face.

"Is that all?" she interrupted with a grin. "That's not a story. Don't you know the rest of the sonnet?"

"Of course." I started to count on my fingers, "The next lines are: 'Well, there's this way and there's that way, and then there's another way.'"

Amanda started to giggle. "Elizabeth Barrett Browning you are not," she said, running her fingernails down my spine. "But I like your version, although I do think you could make it a little more descriptive with your hands and…" she winked at me, "you know."

We stayed in bed for much longer than we had intended that morning.

"I wonder what you look like in a dress," I mused a few mornings later, watching Amanda pulling on her baggy khaki pants. "Do you own such a thing?"

"Of course I do," Amanda sounded pleased at my interest. "I have two dresses with me and a couple of skirts. They're hanging up in your wardrobe. If you are nice to me, I might model them for you one day."

"How about tonight? We could drive into Scourie and have dinner at that new Indian restaurant."

"That sounds lovely," she answered with a smile. "I'll drive and you can pay."

Amanda spent the day roaming the cliffs in search of Albert. I stayed at home to work on a magazine article for a regular client in the Emirates. By mid-morning I was aware that I missed her lively chatter. I wanted to go to the cliffs and find her, instead I went back to work. She came home in the late afternoon, wet and cold, but excited.

"I saw Albert," she told me, as she peeled off her wet socks. "He flew right up in front of me and then he flew in circles, and he was watching me the whole time. It was magical. He seemed to know I wanted him to stay, so he did."

Her enthusiasm was infectious. I let her ramble on for a while before suggesting she warm up with a hot shower. "And put on a skirt, please. Don't forget we are going out tonight."

When she came out of the bedroom much later. I stared at her with my mouth open. "Wow," I managed to comment after a long pause. "You are stunning."

Amanda twirled in front of me wearing black high-heeled shoes and a dark blue dress that stopped just above her knees. As she turned, the skirt fanned out to show her legs to mid thigh. "I thought you already knew that," she laughed. "This is the same me under this flimsy finery."

We almost didn't get to dinner. Amanda put a stop to my advances by saying, "Slow down, mister. This girl hasn't eaten since breakfast. You have to feed me soon, if you want to have your evil way with me later."

Over dinner we talked about Albert. We talked about Amanda's early life. We talked about my expeditions and remote assignments. By unspoken mutual consent, we did not discuss the future.

"I've ridden camels in the Sahara, in Rajasthan, in Saudi Arabia and in the Australian Outback, but I've never ridden a horse," I admitted as we finished the last of the chicken vindaloo. "I'd like to try. Will Djort let me?"

"I don't see why not," Amanda said. "You are familiar to her and she's very gentle. Try a slow ride round the garden in the morning."

I awoke next day to find Amanda fully dressed and offering me a cup of tea. "Time to get up. You have a riding lesson this morning," she announced.

"I thought I had a riding lesson last night, from some wild creature in a blue dress," I groaned.

"Very funny – true, too," Amanda laughed. "Now get up. It's a new day out there."

Her blue dress was still draped in an untidy sprawl across a chair, where one of us had thrown it the night before. I looked at it and started to suggest, "Why don't you put that dress on again and…"

Amanda pulled me out of bed. "No chance," she said. "We are going out. Ask me again this afternoon."

Amanda explained to Djort that I would be riding her this morning. I'm not convinced that the horse understood, but she insisted Djort was intuitive enough to do so.

I'm sure my transition from the ground to the stirrup and then into the saddle was nowhere near as fluid as Amanda's graceful exercise in mounting, but I managed it without falling off and without the horse bolting. That seemed like an achievement to me. We paraded a couple of small circuits without upset. Amanda clapped her hands lightly, stroked Djort on the nose and said, "Good girl. Now, Tripp, try riding her up the hill and down again: slowly, please."

Amanda was leaning against our stone wall when we returned. "You have to relax more," she warned as I dismounted. "You're much too tense. Djort can feel that and it makes her nervous. A rider has to become one with the horse. Your muscles have to flow with hers. Next time, imagine you are out enjoying a stroll with your best friend. Let yourself go; let your body find its own rhythm. Watch me. I'm going to look for Albert."

As Amanda rode away a shadow passed over my head. Looking up I saw Albert Ross doing a tight wingtip turn over the croft. He levelled off, stretched his neck, gave one beat of his powerful wings and followed Amanda and Djort.

"I'm coming," I told the bird. "I'm coming, as soon as I get my equipment."

When I reached my customary Albert-watching site over an hour later and out of breath, Amanda was there; Djort some distance away chomping on the vegetation.

"Albert was just here," she told me. "He's out there now, hunting down in the troughs, but he flew right over my head in a turn. He was watching me again. We made eye contact. That was incredible." Amanda hugged me in her enthusiasm.

"He seems to be in a communicative mood today. He flew a tight circle over the croft just after you rode away. There's no doubt he was watching me, and probably you as well."

"I wonder what he was thinking," we said in unison and laughed with delight.

Amanda chattered into her handheld recorder for five or more minutes, telling it of the latest events. Turning to me as she pocketed the instrument, she said, "I never knew work could be so much fun."

TRIPP & AMANDA

We were comfortable together. We each had our own work 'though the two often overlapped because of Albert Ross. To know him better, we pooled our resources; shared all information. The last of the summer passed with us rarely apart because we were so happy being a couple. Tripp gradually adjusted to my rambunctious ways and I learned to accept his occasional long periods of thoughtful silence. He surprised me on my birthday with a framed portrait of Albert Ross, a lovely card, and a bottle of wine to share.

In late September Tripp received a letter giving him the date and time for his next hospital visit: the one that should give him a new lease on life. The appointment was for early December at the Royal Infirmary of Edinburgh. To celebrate, I gave Tripp a pen and ink sketch of Albert Ross. That day, he finally told me about the mysterious folder marked *Albert and Eddie*. "It's a novella about a lonely, or shy, young boy and an injured albatross he befriends," he explained.

"I assume the lonely little boy is based on you and the albatross is Albert?"

"Not exactly. The book is set in the Falkland Islands before the war with Argentina, but I am certainly drawing on my experiences as a shy boy, and my knowledge of

Albert to build the story." He reached over to a shelf and took down a slim cardboard box. "That folder you saw contained my notes. Here's a copy of the full manuscript. You can read it if you want to. The original has already gone to a publisher."

"You didn't tell me."

"No, I wanted it to be a surprise."

I took the manuscript, curled up in Tripp's armchair by the spluttering fire and read it from the title page to the end. "I think this is a lovely story," I told him a few hours later. I stood up and kissed him. "Thank you, I feel privileged."

"Well, it's another example of my fascination with albatrosses. Do you remember when we first met, I talked about albatrosses carrying the souls of dead mariners?"

"Yes, but, as I said then, that's just fantasy."

"I wonder if it is. I truly believe it's a possibility. Somewhat mystical, I know, but I really do believe it. I would like to think that I would one day be some part of an albatross. Perhaps that's why I'm so fascinated by them."

"But you are not a sailor."

"No, not now, but I was a long time ago. My first job when I left school was as a deckhand on a freighter working the coast of British Columbia. I eventually worked my way up to junior officer status before I settled on land for a while to attend university. Although I never went back to sea in that capacity, as I told you, I later worked on cruise ships as a guest speaker for a few years. I think I qualify as a mariner."

AMANDA

In early November I prepared for a journey to Inverness. For the next few days I would be a teacher, talking to students of all ages about sea birds, their habitats, their lifestyles and their importance in the ecological chain. I also had a doctor's appointment. On the morning of departure I held Tripp tight, saying, "You take care of yourself, and Djort, and Albert. I'll be back in a week."

"Don't worry about us. We'll be fine. You drive carefully, there might be snow in the Highlands. I'll be waiting for you when you get home."

He patted me on the seat of my tight blue jeans as I got into the Land Rover. Closing the door for me, he leaned in for a final kiss and a reminder, "I love you."

I reached out and held his ears – that had become a habit. I studied his craggy face, imprinting it on my memory. "I love you, too. Never forget that."

He watched as I drove away. Changing gears smoothly, despite an attack of nerves, I followed the road past the village. I stopped for a few seconds at the top of the hill and looked back. He was still watching me. I thought about turning the car round. Then, with a growl from the engine, I continued. I couldn't shake a feeling of trouble on the horizon. A nagging doubt inside told me to stay. The teaching job, and my desire for confirmation of that which I suspected, urged me on.

"Oh, well. It's only for a week," I said aloud as I settled back and concentrated on the long journey ahead. "Inverness, here I come."

TRIPP

Each morning while Amanda was away I rode Djort for half an hour on the moors. I spent part of most days walking the cliff-top path, binoculars at the ready, always watching for the albatross, always studying the other birds. I heard gun shots from the grouse hunt on occasion but not close enough to concern me. Alone in the croft for the first time in nearly three months, I was happy enough, even though I missed Amanda's lively personality and constant chatter. I went to bed early and awoke at dawn. In anticipation of Amanda's return, I marked the days off the kitchen calendar as they passed.

Coming down off the cliff in a light drizzle late one afternoon, I passed the postman near the bakery shop.

"I have a letter for you, Mr. Hatcher," he called, reaching into his shoulder bag. "Here it is, all the way from London."

The return address on the thin manila envelope looked ominous enough to make me frown. A rejection, I thought. I opened it anyway and took out a two-page letter. My frown changed to a smile of delight as I read the message. "Oh, yes," I shouted. "That's great!"

"Good news, Mr. Hatcher?"

"You bet, Sandy. It's wonderful news."

I went into the bakery and bought a few bread rolls and a chocolate éclair to celebrate. Sitting at my kitchen table, with a steaming mug of coffee and the éclair for company, I read the opening line of the letter again: *Dear Mr. Hatcher, We would very much like to discuss the possibility of publishing your book...* Those few words, with three more paragraphs of reinforcement, were what I had been waiting for.

"Yes. Oh, yes. Amanda will be excited to see this when she gets home," I told my coffee mug.

AMANDA

I drove out of Inverness on Saturday morning before dawn broke with a smile on my face that stretched from ear to ear. I had thoroughly enjoyed my few days teaching young people about sea birds, and I had a personal triumph.

The old Land Rover wheezed and coughed a few times in the frosty air, but did not falter as we turned onto the road for the distant snow-capped mountains and eventually to home. I wondered what Tripp would say when he heard the news. Would he be excited? Would he be upset? No, I decided. He would definitely be excited for me – for both of us.

Far to the north-west, while my Land Rover was growling its way up and over the hills to reach Loch Broom, Tripp would be waking up. In a few hours, and many miles, I would be able to tell him. Despite the occasional snow on the road and the need for concentration on my driving, I'm sure I smiled all the way home. I felt nothing could intrude on my happiness.

ALBERT

Albert floated on the sea among a flock of squawking gulls, dining on the detritus thrown overboard from a passing fishing boat. Forcing his way through the gulls, Albert began his take off run. He flapped his great wings to get lift, ran across the surface on large webbed feet and launched himself into flight. Airborne, he glided over the waves, changing direction at will with subtle movements of his feathers. Above him on the cliff face, guillemots clung to their nests. A lone gannet soared past, turned on a wingtip and dived into the deep. Albert watched as it surfaced while swallowing a small fish. Feeling an air current, Albert rode it in circles, gradually increasing his altitude towards the top of the cliff.

Up on the nearby moors red grouse scurried through the heather eating seeds, shoots and insects. A line of men and women, preceded by dogs, advanced across the terrain. The people were beaters. Their job was to flush the grouse out of the heather and put them to flight across the sights of the shooters. The dogs were there to retrieve the dead birds.

Albert floated up and up on the current of air. As he crested the top of the cliff, he soared past a covey of fast-flying grouse. The crack of gunfire echoed across the moor. Three grouse fell. Two made their escape. Albert felt a blow on his left wing and that side of his body. The wing went numb. Out of control, he flew in a tight circle and crashed near the cliff-top path.

TRIPP

I awoke feeling lethargic. Not even the anticipation of Amanda's return late in the day could get me motivated. After a while, I rolled out of bed and had a quick wash in cold water before dressing in a pair of faded jeans, grey wool socks and a thick, woollen check shirt. I lit a fire in the hearth before pottering about in the kitchen for a while in a pair of comfortable old carpet slippers. I made a pot of tea and toasted two pieces of whole-wheat bread. On a note pad beside the sink I wrote: eggs, milk, bread, veggies. My breathing was harsh, as it had been occasionally for a few days, and a dull ache invaded my chest. Hoping the symptoms would ease with a bit of exercise, I went to the stable to feed Djort and let her out into the yard. She greeted me with a whinny and a toss of her head. Her upper lip curled back to bare her teeth, anticipating the treat held in my hand.

"Here you are, old girl. An apple for a lady," I stroked the bridge of her proud nose as I placed the first half of a Granny Smith between her teeth. "We won't go riding today, Djort. I'm not feeling my best so I'll go for a short walk instead. Maybe we'll go out later."

Moving slowly, I refilled Djort's hay box and refreshed her drinking trough. I gave her the second half of the apple and watched as she chewed it with a satisfied expression on her face. The dull ache in my chest intensified to a stabbing pain, causing me to stop and lean against a wall. Sweat broke out on my forehead. Feeling dreadful, I staggered back to the croft and downed an aspirin with half a glass of water.

"Damn. I need to rest again," I moaned as I fell into a chair. My eyes closed and my tortured breathing slowed. I felt the sweat cooling on my face and neck as it dried. When I awoke again the morning was more than half over. I was in my armchair and feeling considerably better. I decided to go for a walk.

Strolling along the familiar cliff-top path against a steady drizzle of rain, I began to feel more comfortable with each stride. Determined not to overdo it, I kept to a leisurely pace, my breathing almost normal. My heart rate felt steady. The air was cold, but clear. I felt stronger than I had for days and ready for a few hours studying Albert Ross. My sudden upbeat mood changed in an instant when I saw an untidy pile of black, grey and white feathers sprawled across the path ahead of me in the distance. Hoping I was wrong, I focussed my binoculars on the site. What I saw filled me with agony.

"Oh, no," I heard myself cry. "Oh, no." Holding the binoculars in one hand to prevent them bumping against my chest, I began to run as hard as I could.

AMANDA

There was no one at the croft when I got home in the late afternoon soon after the rain started again. Djort was in her stable, with the top half of the door open. She had fresh straw and a full pail of water. The front door to the house was unlocked, as always. I went in, calling Tripp's name, excited to see him again I went from room to room but there was no one at home.

"Tripp. Tripp, where are you, darling? I have something important to tell you."

A fire burned low in the hearth, the kitchen was tidy with only a few papers stacked on the table. A note about food items needed rested on the kitchen counter. On the dining table, Tripp's laptop was closed. I called out to him again, my voice the only sound. Despite the awful weather, Tripp had obviously gone out although – unusual for him – he had left his camera and tripod in the corner.

"Damn," I said. "Just when I have such incredible news for him. Where on earth could he be?"

After checking that Djort had enough feed, I gave the horse a treat of two sugar cubes and then wandered into the village, head bowed against the wind and a sudden heavy rain shower. I checked the bakery shop first as that was Tripp's favourite stop. There was no sign of him. I ran down the cobblestone street to the small harbour. A brace of fishing boats strained at their moorings. No people were in sight. Maybe I missed him, I thought, if he took a different route home. I knew he would not have gone to Handa. The sea was too rough for a small boat to make the crossing. Instinctively, I looked towards the cliffs where we first met. They were just visible through the driving rain and the fading light.

"Surely he's not out there in this weather," I said out loud.

The village pub was empty. So was the tea shop, and the local garage. I asked a couple of women heading home from shopping, but no one had seen him that day. I returned to the croft but he had not come home. With darkness not far away, I worried that he might be ill somewhere. The wind dropped and the rain slowed to a drizzle. With nowhere else to go, I pocketed a torch and went looking for him on the cliff top path. Rain had made the narrow trail slippery, so I walked a few paces inland through the grass and low heather to avoid falling. Dark clouds scudded overhead, rushing past in the direction of the Orkney Islands.

I found my lover soon after the rain stopped. He sat in the heather close to the edge of the cliff where we had first met. He sat there cradling a black-browed albatross in his arms. Scared of what I might find, I called to him as I approached.

"Tripp. Tripp. I've been searching for you for hours. What's the matter? Are you all right?"

There was no answer. Tripp remained still, the great bird, with wings folded, in his arms. Fearing the worst, I dropped to my knees beside them. Tripp's chin rested on Albert Ross's head. Rainwater trickled down his face and onto the bird's long beak. Tripp's eyes were closed, so were Albert's. Both of them, man and albatross, were cold to my touch.

Hours later, back at the croft after Tripp had been taken away. I laid Albert on a large, thick towel on the kitchen floor and studied him. He had shotgun pellets all along one side of his body and embedded in his fractured left wing.

"Grouse hunters. Damn them," I cried as I began to remove the deadly particles of metal with a pair of tweezers. When I finished, I sat with Albert's body for a while, wondering what to do. There was no one I needed to phone. Tripp had said he didn't have any family. My own parents were away visiting my brother in Bolivia. Tripp had told me months before that he wanted his remains to be cremated and scattered on the sea. Once I had completed a full autopsy on Albert, I decided he would be cremated as well. Somehow, I vowed, I would find a way to scatter their ashes together on the South Atlantic Ocean. Even though we had talked about his heart problems, I had never expected this so soon. It all seemed so dreadfully unfair. We had found each other because of a bird. And now, much too soon, I had lost my lover and the albatross we thought of as ours.

Standing and stretching, I forced myself to make a pot of tea. Then, with a steaming mug in my hand and tears trickling down my face, I began to sort the papers on Tripp's desk. Most were research notes and tear-sheets from articles he had written. His passport, some money and a thick manila envelope – unsealed and unmarked were in a drawer. Inside the envelope were the deeds to the croft, his bank statements and a white envelope addressed to me. Under my name was the inscription – You will know what to do with this when the time comes.

Trying to stop my hands trembling, I opened the envelope and pulled out a few white pages stapled together. The title page read – The Last Will and Testament of Craig Tripp Hatcher.

I sat in Tripp's armchair and read through the pages in sadness and surprise. He had named me as his only beneficiary. I was to receive the title to the croft, all his possessions and the contents of his bank account. If the bank statement attached to the will reflected the true extent of his financial holdings, there was enough money there for me to live comfortably in Scotland for many years. The only proviso in the will was a note to the effect that I must use some of the money to continue my research by going to the Falkland Islands and the waters off Cape Horn to pursue my doctorate. I placed both hands over my still flat belly and held them there, crying bitter, desolate tears. Later, as I was putting the papers away, I noticed a recent addition. On the back of the last page of the will, in Tripp's handwriting, I read, Don't be sad, Amanda. Enjoy your life. See you on the other side, sweetheart. I'll be waiting for you.

"Oh, Tripp, my darling," I wept, "if only you could have stayed a little longer. I had such wonderful news for you."

ALBERT
&
AMANDA
&
TRIPP

The cliff on the north-west side of Saunders Island rippled with energy as hundreds of black-browed albatrosses settled; made themselves comfortable on their carefully constructed conical earthen nests. Some, a few dozen, rode the air currents off shore, their great wings hardly moving – nothing more than a subtle adjustment of strategic feathers – as they cruised past the rugged rock faces of the bleak north coast of the Falkland Islands.

Amanda stood in silence at the edge of the colony. She scanned the nesting birds, her eyes roaming from left to right and back again. She appeared to be counting the flock. When she raised her sights, she became aware of two birds watching her. At first, they were stationary, holding position on the wind a short distance away from the cliff. Together they wheeled away, making a large circuit behind her and back out to sea again. Changing direction, they cruised in from the north, flying wing tip to wing tip. They matched each other's casual movements, never quite touching but never more than the space of a man's hand between them. They flew past Amanda at eye level, the nearest no more than a wingspan away from her. As one, they circled, changing positions so that the outer bird on the first pass was now closest to

Amanda. They passed again, keeping perfect formation, their heads inclined towards her, their eyes on hers.

Amanda laughed with delight. Placing one hand under the bump growing in her body and the other above it to emphasize the gentle rounded shape, she turned sideways to the two albatrosses as they came around for another pass. The giant birds came closer this time, so close she could almost reach out and touch them. The nearest bird nodded its head slowly as it looked at her profile. The pair circled, changing positions again as they turned for another pass. Amanda felt tears of joy trickling down her cheeks and she nodded in unison with the birds as they appeared to acknowledge the child within her.

One more time the pair circled, maintaining their tight formation, wing tip to wing tip. They passed Amanda again at eye level. As one they rocked their wings from side to side in gentle accord. Then, just when she thought they would come past again, they soared, gaining height quickly as they rode a current of warmer air. High above the cliffs where Amanda stood on the edge of the nesting colony, the two albatrosses turned west and south, heading out over the ocean where she had scattered the ashes of her two loves only days before.

"They're going to Cape Horn and the Southern Ocean," Amanda said quietly, shading her eyes with one hand. She watched until the two great birds dwindled to specks and then disappeared.

"They're going to Cape Horn," she said, louder this time and with a laugh in her voice. "Tripp and Albert are going home."

The end

AUTHOR'S NOTE AND ACKNOWLEDGEMENTS

This book is a work of fiction loosely based on a real black-browed albatross that roamed the north-west coast of Scotland for many years. I must emphasize that all human characters in this story are fictional only. They are products of my imagination and any resemblance to persons, living or dead, is entirely unintentional.

A huge THANK YOU to naturalist Graham Sunderland of Vancouver, B.C., Canada. Graham told me about the real Albert Ross while we were watching albatrosses skimming between the waves of the Southern Ocean off Cape Horn when we were both guest speakers on board the cruise ship *Celebrity Infinity* in early 2013. Thanks to the enrichment staff at Celebrity Cruises in Miami who sent me on that and many similar exotic voyages all over the world to entertain their passengers.

Don Enright, friend, neighbour, ornithologist, wildlife photographer, public speaker and professional naturalist, checked my facts about the birds mentioned in this book and corrected me where I had strayed from reality. I am indebted to him. Any errors that remain are mine.

A special thank you must go to Tripp Hatch, an excellent bartender in the United Airlines Club lounge at the George Bush Intercontinental Airport in Houston, Texas. Tripp Hatch gave me permission to borrow his unusual name for this book. It is a special name. I am honoured to have used it.

Once again, my gratitude goes to my best friend Steve Crowhurst for pushing me to finish this story and for designing the book's cover. And, of course, thanks as always to my first readers: Steve, Penny, Don, Shirley. This book is better for your eagle eyes (perhaps that should be albatross eyes?).

The two lines of love poetry misquoted by the fictional Tripp Hatcher are borrowed from *Sonnet 43* by Elizabeth Barrett Browning, one of my early literary influences. Although I have played with them, those words are used with the utmost respect. The song that Amanda tried to remember was *People Will Say We're In Love*, from *Oklahoma*, by Rodgers & Hammerstein. It too is mentioned with respect.

My appreciation goes to all those who buy and read my books, both fiction and non-fiction. I write for all of you.

Also by Anthony Dalton

Fiction
The Sixth Man
The Mathematician's Journey
Relentless Pursuit

Non-fiction
Portraits of Bangladesh
Henry Hudson
Sir John Franklin
Fire Canoes
The Fur-Trade Fleet
Polar Bears
Adventures with Camera and Pen
A Long, Dangerous Coastline
Graveyard of the Pacific
Arctic Naturalist, the life of J. Dewey Soper
River Rough, River Smooth
Alone Against the Arctic
Baychimo, Arctic Ghost Ship
J/Boats Sailing to Success
Wayward Sailor, in Search of the Real Tristan Jones

For more about Anthony Dalton and his books,
visit his website at

www.anthonydalton.net
www.themathematiciansjourney.com

ABOUT THE AUTHOR

Anthony Dalton is a Fellow of the Royal Geographical Society and a Fellow of the Royal Canadian Geographical Society. He is the award-winning author of 15 non-fiction books, most about the sea or about exploration, and three earlier novels. A past President of the Canadian Authors Association, and an accomplished public speaker, he is an historian and a former expedition leader. He lives in the Southern Gulf Islands of British Columbia, Canada, with his wife Penny and a yellow Labrador named Rufus.

81123286R00104

Made in the USA
Columbia, SC
25 November 2017